Created Worlds

CREATED WORLDS

A SHORT STORY COLLECTION

JOAN MARIE VERBA

FTL PUBLICATIONS
MINNEAPOLIS, MINNESOTA

FTL Publications
P O Box 22693
Minneapolis, MN 55422-0693
www.ftlpublications.com
mail@ftlpublications.com

Cover art by Joe Prachatree

ISBN 978-1-936881-51-2

Publishing history

"The Wisest Wizard," *Mythic Circle* 32, June 2010
"The Sum of the Parts," *Science Fiction Review*, Summer 1991
"Safe Passage" was originally published in the Darkover anthology *Snows of Darkover*, January 1995. Reprinted by permission.
"The Madwoman of the Kilghard Hills" (retitled here as "The Mystery Woman of the Kilghard Hills") was originally published in the Darkover anthology *Towers of Darkover*, July 1993. Reprinted by permission.
"An Invitation to Chaos" was originally published in the Darkover anthology *Leroni of Darkover*, November 1991. Reprinted by permission.
"The Honor of the Guild" was originally published in the Darkover anthology *Renunciates of Darkover*, March 1991. Reprinted by permission.
"Mind-eater" was originally published in the Darkover anthology *Domains of Darkover*, March 1990. Reprinted by permission.
"Death's Scepter" was originally published in the Darkover anthology *Four Moons of Darkover*, November 1988. Reprinted by permission.
"This One Time" was originally published in the Darkover anthology *Free Amazons of Darkover,* December 1985. Reprinted by permission.

TABLE OF CONTENTS

The Wisest Wizard

Penelope had staged the most beautiful funeral I had ever seen. In the glade, the apple trees remained in blossom, and a subtle spicy fragrance enriched the air. Bright sunlight streamed through the leaves. Birds of paradise trilled melodically. The bier carrying Penelope's body—gorgeously arrayed—floated down the aisle created by the seated mourners. Impressive trick, that: getting an article to levitate took months of preparation, and the magic could be executed by only the most powerful of wizards. Of course, Penelope had been The Wise Wizard, but even so, it must have taken years for her to set the spells and time them to work after she had taken her last breath. No doubt she had entrusted her assistant, Adele, walking behind the bier, with the word or gesture to set it all in motion.

I looked around at the spectators, wondering who would become the next Wise One. Sylvia, the obvious choice, had contracted a fever and lay abed at home, sick. Her assistant, Freya, had told Daphne and me that Sylvia had at first shunned the healing potions—which would send her into a long, deep sleep—and attempted to get out of bed twice to come to the funeral. Both times, she had collapsed on the doorstep. Freya had been spared the effort to carry her back to bed—the swordswoman was almost as old as Sylvia was—because of the numerous visitors who had come by and had given Freya a hand. (After the second fainting spell, Sylvia had yielded to Freya's pleas and sipped the medicine.) The visitors all said that they had come to see if Sylvia needed any extra care in her illness; but Daphne told me they came, rather, to see if Sylvia was shamming. Daphne assured me, after we left the wizard's cottage, that Sylvia was not shamming.

Who, then, would replace Penelope? Lola, who had only recently been shown the door by her wizard mentor after her journeyman elevation, was young, but ambitious. Daphne told me Lola might make the attempt, but becoming the Wise One required a certain amount of maturity and experience that Lola had yet to achieve. The only others I could see who had both the desire and the ability to carry out the test were Metis or Urania—and of course, Daphne.

I had assisted Daphne for 17 years now. The common people think that wizards use apprentices to assist them, but in reality, the apprentices are too incompetent and hot-headed to assist until they are able to complete their journeyman tasks, and after that, they're shown the door (with great ceremony and hearty congratulations, of course, but nonetheless, they're out). No, wizards generally choose their assistants from the ranks of women-at-arms. They find us to be seasoned, reliable, and eager—most eager, because the food is good, the pay is outstanding, and the accommodations are cozy. I had not experienced the dubious pleasure of standing at a cold, dank watch post in the pre-dawn hours for quite some time.

I turned my attention back to the funeral. The bier had reached the front of the assembly and turned. Penelope lay there peacefully, dressed in her finest wizard silks (green and gold), her wrinkled face showing an aged beauty that reflected the selfless deeds she had joyfully pursued in life. I would miss her cheerful demeanor. Slowly, as I watched, body, clothes, and bier dissolved into dust that sparkled in the sun—one final brilliant touch from The Wise Wizard.

Daphne tapped my arm, her usual way of drawing my attention. "Let's go, Isabel," she said softly. I nodded and followed her. I already saw that Lola and her assistant, Radnir, had gone, as had Metis and Esme, Urania and Nyla. The others remained in the glade and gathered to talk, probably about us. Being The Wise Wizard meant having an honorable title, and possession of the ancient artifacts from the dawn of time, allowing the owner to perform the most powerful and intricate spells known. But the ancient artifacts themselves had been bound with a spell before the dawn of time. Once the current Wise One died, they hid themselves, and no one but a wizard pure in heart could find and use them. Even then, the finding would be risky and dangerous, and not many wizards would take on the pursuit. Indeed, most found the very idea a foolish one.

"Pure in heart"—aye, that was a mouthful. I told Daphne on one occasion, when I was feeling brave, that I did not think I ever met anyone who was truly pure in heart. Daphne, who seemed not in the least insulted by my remark, explained that perfection was not required, else no mortal could take them. Rather, she said, the accumulation of selfless deeds left an imprint on the soul much as an accumulation of selfish deeds left a stain on the soul. The preponderance of selfless deeds, no matter what mortal errors one may make in life, would make a soul shine as the moon on a clear night.

Sylvia possessed such a soul. Everyone expected that once Penelope died, that Sylvia would be drawn to the ancient artifacts—and they to her—as metal to a lodestone. Still, a wizard did have to exert some effort to find the artifacts, and it was clear that Sylvia could not walk out her front door. Daphne, and apparently others, felt the artifacts too important to be left untouched until Sylvia regained her strength.

In my estimation, Daphne was the strongest candidate among the other seekers. She was honest, truthful, and caring. She trained apprentice after apprentice who left her home and honorably served the ladies and lords in their estates, making sure the babies (human and animal) were sound of health and grew strong and wise. None of Daphne's apprentices, to our knowledge, had ever used magic for power or gain. Daphne, however, did not have the seniority, and therefore, the experience of a wizard such as Sylvia.

Metis, a skilled and precise wizard, nonetheless had the disadvantage of growing up unloved. A need to prove her worthiness continually drove her to accomplish great and noble deeds, but her upbringing meant her deeds lacked warmth. She could be pleasant, but her manner often seemed harsh, particularly when she was frustrated, simply because no one had ever bothered to teach her manners (and whenever anyone tried, they found themselves the objects of her frustration, and quickly gave up). Other wizards, as well as other common folk, avoided her for those reasons, making her feel more rejected and driving her further to prove that she was worthy of being included in society. I (and Daphne) had no doubt she saw becoming the Wise One as a way to finally be included and loved.

Urania, on the other hand, had become the most social of butterflies. Everyone loved to see her coming—until one of her whims took over. Then visitors could find that their ale had suddenly turned to water, or water to ale. To Urania, this was harmless buffoonery, and because of her affable manner, she easily received forgiveness. No one suspected that Urania would ever use the ancient artifacts for anything evil, but Daphne, for one, could easily see that with them, a colossal joke could turn into a colossal mess.

Without Sylvia's brilliant integrity, the best that the others could do in the search was to check the most potent centers of magic (the wizards' country was defined as the territory where these magical centers were found) in the hopes that the artifacts would be drawn to them, as they had in the past. Nothing was more potent in magic—and more dangerous to life and limb— than a firedrake's lair; I quickly saw that Daphne was headed to the nearest one. I loosened my sword in its sheath. Firedrakes were notoriously hard to kill; nonetheless, over the eons, men had hunted them for sport, and now only a handful of families lived in wizards' country. I did not wish to kill one, but I was not going to let one harm me or Daphne, either.

Daphne glanced back, seeing my gesture. "You won't need that. I've set protective spells for us."

"Just being prepared."

Daphne stopped at the edge of a clearing—the border between the forest and the mountains. I could smell burnt twigs and leaves, as well as a faint odor of sulfur. Before us yawned a huge cave mouth. At the top of the cave, peering over the rocks, we could see Metis and Esme. To our left, again, where forest met rocks, stood Lola and Radnir. Urania and Nyla stood just beyond them.

All of us watched the firedrakes. The father, resplendent in shining orange and silver scales, used his nose to scratch at the joints where his stubby legs and wormy torso met. The mother, all silver and no orange, lovingly nosed the five offspring in her nest—imps, we called the little ones. I saw 3 males and 2 females. With their heads held high, the imps were about as tall as my shoulder; they weighed almost twice as much as I did. The nest they played in consisted of jewels and mud that the adult firedrakes had used their fiery breath to harden.

The jewels resembled opals or diamonds, but actually they were rocks or crystals, eaten and digested by the firedrakes, who ate anything—animal, vegetable, or mineral. Somehow the process of digestion imbued the stones with magic. Daphne once attempted to explain how the solids absorbed the magic that animated the firedrakes, but I was a little too fastidious to pay much attention. Daphne had magical firedrake stones, and assured me they were entirely clean from being burned by the firedrake's breath (after the firedrake deposited the droppings), and washed, just to be on the safe side, but I was reluctant to handle them, nonetheless.

The firedrake stones varied in magical power. Some had very weak power; I had seen Daphne put them in a cradle to ease a babe's tooth pains. Others had tremendous power; Daphne said the most potent could bring down a mountain, or even better, could cause an object or objects to disappear from one location and reappear at another. But those were rare and only a wizard could scry one to see how much power any of them had. Generally wizards got the stones by visiting an abandoned nest, but one hardly found any of those in these times. The stones Daphne or any other wizard had were few, and old.

I saw a motion to my left. Radnir held up a large melon and motioned to the imps. "Here, baby, come here, see what I've got!"

I rolled my eyes. It appeared that Lola wanted Radnir to lure an imp to her. The other imps would follow, and the parents would come to be sure the imps came to no harm. Then Lola would search the cave while the firedrakes were distracted. Again, that seemed to be the plan, but it was a bad one—even if they had magical Roc bird feathers to protect them from injury, this would not prevent a firedrake from grabbing or trapping them.

Radnir and Lola could not have anticipated what happened next. The first imp left the nest and ran straight to Radnir, amazingly fast. The other imps rushed forward at a breakneck pace, tackling not only Lola and Radnir, but Urania and Nyla as well, rolling them playfully on the ground. The parents scuttled over to supervise, trumpeting encouragement.

Daphne shook her head. "They'll live—they're well protected, but they're not going anywhere for a while." She took a drawstring bag out of her own shoulder sack and threw it to me. "Gather all the stones you can. I'm going to search the cave." She ran into the cave, kindling a handlight as she went, while I searched around the nest for anything that looked magical and clean. I had almost filled up the bag when I felt a nudge on my arm.

"One moment, I'm almost done."

"Who are you talking to?"

I looked up to see Daphne standing in front of me. Then who nudged me? I turned to find an imp cooing at me. Its breath was uncomfortably warm, and smelled of melon. Without thinking, I picked up a nearby rock and tossed it at the imp. The imp caught it with its mouth and began crunching it.

"Don't feed it!" said Daphne. "It'll follow us!"

"But...."

The damage done, she rolled a large piece of quartz in its direction to keep it there a few moments more. She touched my arm. "After me."

I always did exactly what Daphne said, even if it made no sense to me at the time. I learned the hard way that Daphne knew what she was doing even if I did not. And it did not make sense that Daphne was running to where the other imps were still rolling the women, apparently amused by the noises they made. We ran uncomfortably close to Father Firedrake's legs, and into the forest. Daphne stopped next to a tree, turned, and made a motion as if throwing a rock a long distance. A tongue of fire sprouted up by the nest. The imp I had fed screamed, and the other firedrakes raced back to the nest.

"You didn't hurt it?" I asked. One less firedrake meant even fewer firedrake stones.

"No, imps scream with excitement when they see fire."

The other women were badly shaken and had grass and twigs and pebbles in their hair and clothes, but they were largely unhurt. After helping them to the nearest forest path, Daphne and I left them there to gather their wits again.

Once we were a safe distance from the other women, I handed Daphne my bag. "This is all I could get."

She took it but did not open it. "I'm sure they're fine. Any firedrake stone will have a use."

"Did you find the ancient artifacts in the cave?"

She shook her head. "But I found a number of firedrake stones."

"Powerful ones?"

"I won't know that until I'm able to get home and examine them."

"I don't think that Urania or Lola will become The Wise One."

"No, it will be some time before they fully recover their senses. They're only barely capable of walking home as it is."

"What now?"

"I'm going to check on Sylvia and then go home."

"You're giving up on seeking the ancient artifacts? Aren't you afraid that Metis will get them?"

Daphne smiled. "Metis knows less than she thinks. I'll be more useful against her if I work my magic from home, at least for now. You'll continue the search."

"You have great confidence in me," I said, implying with my tone that the confidence might not be merited.

"I do," she said with a grin.

Daphne left a small firedrake stone on Sylvia's blanket; Sylvia had not awakened, Freya said, since we had last been there.

My next task, Daphne told me before we parted, was to climb the Tower Tree. That, too, contained a magical center, and attracted Rocs, which nested in the highest branches. I stood at the base of the tree—as wide as a cottage—and considered my path upward. I could not see the top through the myriad branches and countless leaves, but I heard rustling and the cry of a Roc. If one caught me with its beak or claws, I could be its dinner. Still, with the tree so large, I could conceivably get up to the top without the Roc or I ever setting eyes on the other.

I started the climb. I would ascend about the height of a city wall, rest a few minutes, and go up again. The Roc screamed every now and again, but I knew from the sound I remained at a safe distance.

Once I was high enough to view the entire valley, I heard a heavy rustling—too heavy for a squirrel or bird of paradise, many of which I had already seen. But it was not loud enough to be a Roc, either. I craned my neck to look up. Identifying the source of the sound, I called out. "Well met, Esme. What are you doing here?"

"The same thing you're doing here, presumably," she called down. "I see you survived the firedrakes."

"Quite nicely, thank you," I said. "Daphne set magical wards to protect us."

She nodded. "Metis determined the ancient artifacts weren't there and we should move on."

I refrained from asking how Metis knew that without making a search, as Daphne had. Wizards generally did not tell their assistants such secrets, and even when they did, assistants generally would not share them with other assistants. "Is she with you?"

"No. I need to get a Roc feather for a magic spell, and then move on."

That told me that Metis did not think the ancient artifacts were here, either. If so, I should move on, too. But perhaps Metis was wrong and they were here. I kept climbing. Esme did too, but went to the other side of the tree, out of my sight. I kept an eye out for Rocs, but did not see any. Eventually, I came to a hole in the tree. I knew it to be a magical locus due to the lack of bird or squirrel droppings. The hole was large enough for me to grasp the edge with my gloved hands and pull myself inside. Cracks in the bark let in some sunlight, but I saw nothing but...Roc feathers. Drifted down from the nests and pulled in by the tree's magic, I guessed. I pulled out a handful and sat on the branch with my back to the trunk, considering. I would take them with me—since they were magical, Daphne would find a use for them. I placed them inside my vest. But should I tell Esme, to spare her a dangerous encounter with the giant bird? As I pondered this question, I looked out over the valley. Who should I see, but Metis walking along the forest path to... the enchanted pool. When I looked down to contemplate my path to the ground, I saw Esme descending beneath me. I almost laughed. Misdirected! Metis and Esme were nothing if not clever.

An unearthly screech startled me, causing me to nearly lose my balance. A Roc hovered near me, peering at me, screaming at me. Fortunately, the branches and foliage were so thick in this part of the tree that it could not reach me, though it lashed out with beak and claws, tearing at the leaves and smaller outer branches. As long as I stayed close to the trunk, I ought to make it to the ground safely. With the feathers in my jacket, it could not harm me, but it could grab me if it got close enough. Sure enough, once the Roc got too low to maintain its flight—a Roc could not fly from the ground, it had to stay in the heights—it gave up and ascended to its nest.

Even with the head start, Metis and Esme could do little at the enchanted pool before I got there. A den of snakes guarded the grottoes, and I knew neither of them could swim well. I, on the other hand, had been an expert swimmer from my youth, and practiced charming magical snakes long before I ever met Daphne. Besides, I had Roc feathers in my jacket.

Once I hit the ground and cleared the tree, I looked up just to make sure the Roc was not about to swoop down on me. But I saw it circling in the distance, apparently intent on other prey. I turned and took the path to the pool. I did not immediately see Metis or Esme, but they could be behind any of the rock formations. They were not the objects of my search, in any case. I knelt and pounded on the ground. Soon after, a snake appeared, thick as my arm, long as I was high. It slithered to my hand. I allowed it to taste and smell my fingers with its forked tongue, then I stroked it under the jaw. Now it was my friend. I picked it up and carried it underneath the rocky overhang, and set it at the edge of the pool. It would attack anyone else who came near.

Daphne had taken me here before. Wizards often used the pool to store objects because of the snake guardians, and because the pool's own enchantments made it easy to set spells. One lingering spell allowed a swimmer's clothes to stay dry while in the pool. I counted on that as I took off my boots, stepped in the main pool, and sank. I still had to hold my breath but did not have to do that long. The first shelf was not far. I surfaced, looked, and found that empty. I drew breath again, sank, and surfaced at another location. I only put my head and arms above water. Learning on the shelf with my arms, I saw some magical objects, but ordinary ones, not the ancient artifacts. Searching further, I found two other empty areas, and three areas filled with more objects. I almost submerged again at the third area when something caught my eye. At first glance, these had appeared to be ordinary magical objects, similar to the ones in the shelves I had seen in Daphne's and every other wizard's dwelling I had ever entered: a crystal globe, a walking staff, a wooden bowl, among other items. But as I gazed at them, they seemed to take on...a glamour, a sanctity. These were the ones! I had found them! I tentatively reached for them, then drew my hand back. Should I touch them? Perhaps I should just leave them and report my find to Daphne. As I mulled over the options in my mind, the objects dissolved before my eyes.

I blinked. No! They had been there. I would have sworn it. Now they were...gone? How? This I had better report to Daphne.

I swam back to the main pool and surfaced. As I climbed out of the water, I saw Metis sitting on a stone bench, stuffing a wooden bowl into an almost-full pouch. Esme stood beside her. I looked toward my snake friend. He coiled there still, asleep.

"Wizards are even better at charming snakes," Metis observed.

I sat on a rock, speechless.

Metis stood. "You needn't worry. I'm not going to use these to steal, or conquer territory. I just want to be recognized for my genuine abilities. Now everyone will have to agree that I'm not the worthless wretch they thought I was." She left the grotto, Esme following.

I trudged back to Daphne's cottage, wondering what I should say. To forestall explaining the painful details, I first showed Daphne the Roc feathers.

Her face brightened. "Oh, Roc feathers. I can't have too many of those." She took them and put them away, then she turned to me again. "Did you see the ancient artifacts?"

Startled, I simply said, "Yes."

She said excitedly, "You must tell me what they look like."

I shrugged. "You can probably ask Metis."

Daphne picked up a firedrake jewel and held it to the window, to the light. "Oh, she doesn't know."

"But she has them."

Daphne smiled. "She thinks she does. She knows less than she thinks."

I gasped. "Did you get them after all?" I said eagerly.

She laughed—not mocking me, but expressing joy. "No, Sylvia has them."

"Sylvia?"

"Yes, she recovered enough to claim them."

I remembered the firedrake stone that Daphne had left on Sylvia's blanket. It must have healed her, awakened her from slumber. "But Metis has...?"

"Ordinary magical artifacts, from one of the other shelves in the grotto. Well, not so ordinary, they're rather powerful, but nothing she can't be trusted with."

I considered that. I did see more than one wooden bowl in the grotto. Metis must have taken one of those, mistaking a very potent artifact for an ancient artifact.

Daphne held up the jewel in her hand. "But what I have here has an even greater power than anything Metis gathered."

"What is it?"

"Something that I think will affect Metis for the better. She thinks that she can earn love through acts of courage, when she needs to add acts of kindness. It may change Urania, too. She will be easier to live with once she knows that she doesn't have to trick people to get their attention." She put the jewel down. "Some barriers are almost impossible to break, even with magic. But this jewel can help people understand themselves better."

I gestured to the jewels. "They can do all that."

She put down the one in her hand. "With the proper care and attention, this one can." She waved a hand over all the other accumulated jewels. "We collected quite a cache, you and I. There are some exceedingly powerful stones among these."

"You don't mind Sylvia getting the ancient artifacts?"

"Not at all." She picked up another jewel and held it to the light. "When Sylvia reaches the end of her natural life, I think we will be ready." She turned to me with a cheerful expression. Exactly how I would expect the next Wise One to act.

The Sum of the Parts

Susan Page's eye scanned the room. It was a typical hospital room: sound-absorbent tiles on the ceiling, walls, and floor, a monitor by the bedside, a bedside stand, a bed. Page awakened, head fogged by drugs and shock, right eye moving without her conscious control. She squinted to get the device back in line, and turned both eyes toward her right arm. As she feared, it was gone from the elbow down. In its place was a cybernetic arm. She wriggled its fingers. It worked.

"I see you're awake," said Dr. Halsey, in his Boston accent, as he hovered over the bed.

Page scratched her nose with her new fingers.

"Good," said Halsey. "I think that's going to work out fine. You can probably leave tomorrow. Just take it easy for a few days, and try not to get shot again for a while."

Page raised her right eyebrow.

"Want me to adjust the eye for you so it won't look around while you're asleep?"

"No, it's OK. Thanks."

"No problem. I'll check back later. Buzz the kitchen when you get hungry." He indicated a panel on the bedside table.

Page nodded to show she had heard.

Halsey walked out, nearly colliding with a man in a business suit.

"OK if I come in?" he asked Halsey.

Halsey glanced at Page. "It's all right with me if it's all right with her."

"In that case..." The man stepped inside.

Halsey backed into the corridor, pointing to the man. "You could still stand to lose a little weight, Lt. Futura."

"Muscle. It's all muscle."

Halsey shook his head and walked away.

Futura took out a bag of Potato Snax from inside his suit coat. He tilted it at Page. "Want some?"

"No thanks."

He pulled the fastener at the top and poured out the popcorn-sized potato chips in his hand. "Mending well?"

"S'pose so."

"You know, if the law didn't require us to investigate every shooting, we'd have given up on you by now. I've taken to duplicating my previous reports, and filling in a new date and site of injury."

"Captain tired of sending you here?"

"Hell, no. We've got a pool on you over at the station, picking dates when Collins will shoot you next. The Captain won this one."

"Oh? Put me down in the pool for Saturday."

Futura laughed. Particles of Potato Snax bounced on his tongue. "I thought you'd get a charge out of that. I put money on the slot where it says he doesn't shoot you. I haven't won yet, but some day I might. I'm a sucker for long odds."

Page said nothing. She felt tired. She wiggled her new fingers again.

The policeman put his bag down and took out his book-sized computer notepad. "I already got the place of the shooting from the paramedic that picked you up. Did Collins do or say anything unusual this time?"

"No, he just said, 'Hey, Page, over here,' and shot me."

Futura put the notepad away. "Still going to stick with the Pacifists League?"

"What do you think?"

He shook his head. "I still think you ought to get a gun. No one's going to deny you a permit, with your record. He ain't going to give up. The fact that you won't fight back just attracts him. He's that sort of guy."

"It has to start somewhere."

He picked up his snack bag. "I admire your principles, but pacifists just don't get on in a world like this."

"If not here, where?"

He shrugged. "I'll call you if we catch him, but don't count on it."

* * *

The next day, as she sat on a bench in the hospital entryway, waiting for her ride, she heard a patient arguing with a doctor. The sounds came from the nearby emergency wing.

"But I tell you, I just have to have a jacked-up arm."

"Sorry, but it will take a police order to get an enhanced prosthesis."

"I'll pay you for it. I'11 pay big."

"You're about 20 years too late, friend. We aren't paid by patients anymore. We' re paid by the government, in case you hadn't noticed. I'm not about to lose my license by violating their rules."

"Then I'll go elsewhere! I'll go to Russia! They'll take my money!"

"Don't bump your butt on the way out the door."

Page heard a snort. A man stomped out of the emergency wing. His left arm was a cybernetic one, same as hers.

A soft "meep" caught her attention. Mark Ashcroft was outside. Page stood, shouldered her bag, brushed some lint off her khaki pants, and walked to the car. She got in the passenger's side. The engine swished into life and they drove off.

Ashcroft glanced over at her. "Nice arm."

"It'll do."

"What did the police say?"

"Same as always. I ought to get a gun and shoot him."

"Anytime you want, you can borrow mine."

She glared at him.

"Sorry." He smiled. "I respect your beliefs and all, but I don't think that you're obligated to stand around and let this guy shoot you."

"Can you think of a tactic that I haven't tried?"

"What about changing your identity and going someplace else?"

Page shook her head. "People like Collins are all over. If I went somewhere else, I'd have the same problem."

"What do other Pacifist Leaguers do? What does the head of your outfit say?"

"Since we're fairly new, no one has had a problem quite like mine yet. Harassment—habitual harassment—yes; multiple shootings, no. You know I've tried everything else: avoiding him, confronting him, talking to him, pairing with someone else, changing residences, going on an extended vacation..." She sighed. "If you think of something else, let me know."

"If it were someone gunning for me, I'd grab my gun and shoot him first."

"That's what makes the murder rate what it is today."

He shrugged. "Got to survive, any way you can." He stopped the car. "Want me to walk you to your room?"

"No, I can make it. Collins probably won't try to shoot me again for a while." She got out of the car. He went to put it in the garage. Page had a car, too, but since an ambulance had brought her to the hospital, hers was still in the garage.

The apartment in which they both lived was a four-story brick building. She walked up the stairs to her second floor apartment. The bare wooden floor had one area rug in the middle. There was one bookshelf, a rocking chair, couch, television, and a computer on her desk. Her bedroom had the bed and one set of drawers. She wondered how, in a life of 32 years, she had accumulated so little. At least it allowed her to save for retirement, that is, if she should live long enough to do so.

On the wall was a framed wedding portrait of her and her late husband, killed by crossfire after 14 months of marriage while coming home from the cleaners. Page had joined the Pacifist League even before the funeral. The newspapers picked up the story and published a picture of her as she was taking the oath at the local League headquarters. The day after the funeral, Collins shot her for the first time; she lost her leg. The media picked up on that, too, even showing Collins's old mug shot. Collins had plastic surgery before trying again. The police asked the media to stop showing Collins's picture, so that he would not keep changing his features.

She looked again at herself in her wedding dress. "You wouldn't recognize me now, Scott," she said to the image of her husband. She slung her purse strap over a chair and sat on the couch. She cradled her head in the palm of her new hand, thrumming her fingers on her cheek. Flesh-and-blood fingers felt nicer, but she could get used to it, as she had gotten used to her new right eye, her new left leg (below the knee), the reconstructed hip, the artificial ear, the right half-foot, the left breast implant, the prosthetic shoulder socket, the ceramic jaw, and the mechanical left thumb.

Futura came around again while Page was at work. Page had a job at a local TV station, maintaining the equipment—cameras, computers, and such, and doing odd jobs around the place. Her employers were understanding about the amount of sick time she had been using, especially since others could fill in while she was out, but Page wondered if and when she would reach the limit of their good will.

The policeman walked in while she was putting up the set on an empty sound stage, making sure that the desks and chairs and props were where the director wanted them. He watched as she worked to screw two metal tubes together to make a tall light pole, and said, "You know, with this sort of job, you ought to put a special strength enhancer on that arm."

Page set the fixture down. "Don't you need a police permit for that sort of thing?"

He cocked his head to one side. "Nah, not with your kind of job. We let construction workers and such put them on all the time. Here, I got the tools in my trunk." Before she could take a breath, he was out the door.

Minutes later, he came back, and put a tool box on one of the tables. "I worked my way through college as a cybernetic repairman. Did this all the time. Still keep the tools around …never know when they'll come in handy." Carefully, he took off his suit coat, folded it, and laid it on the back of a chair. He sat and opened the kit. "Here, put your arm down."

She sat across from him and laid her right arm on the table. He took various pieces out of his tool box, laid them next to the girders and gears in the arm to see if they fit, and used his tools to add them to the assembly.

"You know," she said, "if I put my hand around someone's throat with an enhanced arm, I could strangle them in an instant."

He glanced up at her, tongue pressed to the side of his mouth as if it was helping him in the effort. "You don't say."

"I've heard that some cybernetic limbs can crush steel. You wouldn't be enhancing it to that level, would you?"

"If I were, I wouldn't tell you about it."

"If I thought my limbs would kill someone without my conscious participation, I'd get them replaced, you know."

"Nah, I'm not going that far." Still puttering with his tools, he added, "Tell me something. If you wore bullet proof armor, and the bullet ricocheted off it and killed the shooter, would that violate your League oath?"

"Not at all. That would be considered the shooter's fault."

"Ever consider getting some?"

"How do you think I lost my eye?"

"Oh. Yeah, that happened before I was transferred here and got your case." He put his fingers into her arm assembly and twisted something into place. "There. Finished." He closed his tool kit. "Remember what Halsey told you: don't use the cybernetic arm to lift anything you wouldn't lift with your flesh-and-blood arm, or your artificial one could drop off. But you can give one hell of a handshake if you want to."

She flexed her fingers. "I'll remember. Thanks."

He picked up his suit coat and put it back on. "Try putting another of those fixtures together." When she had done so, much faster than before, he added, "Easier, isn't it?"

She nodded.

He pointed. "Try removing that teeny tiny screw with your fingers. You should have the dexterity of a pickpocket, though I don't recommend going into the profession."

She tried it. It came out faster than if she had used a tool to remove it.

"Oh." He took out his computer notepad. "Almost forgot why I came. Our informants tell us that Collins hasn't changed his features since shooting you last, though I suppose that eye of yours can't be fooled by simple surgery. Of course, he still doesn't stay twenty minutes in any given spot. But if we catch him, we'll let you know."

It was dark. Collins was there. His arm reached up with his gun, as it had so many times before, aimed point-blank at her. She used her new arm to grab the wrist with the gun. She turned it away from her and squeezed. He dropped the gun. She kept squeezing. She heard the bones crack. He screamed. She laughed. The arm went to his neck. It closed. She could not stop it. did not want to stop it. The veins burst from his skin. He choked on his own blood. The man died, hanging from her clenched fingers, covered with gore.

She sat up in bed with a gasp. The fingers of her right hand were separated, relaxed, as they were on her flesh-and-blood hand. She did have control.

The vidiphone rang. She pulled aside the covers and went to the living room in her nightgown. The picture on the receiver was blank; there was sound only.

"Susan?" said a strained voice.

"What is it, Rita?"

"Can you come over right now? Tom got shot. He's in the hospital, and they say he'll be all right, but I don't know what to do."

"Stay calm, Rita, I'll be right over. Listen, I'm going to hang up and call you again just to be sure this is you. The last time I got a call at 2 a.m. it was Collins and I got shot."

Click.

Page slammed the receiver shut and kicked the desk for good measure. Collins, again. Ready to shoot her, again. Time to make plans, again. She sighed. If she got through this, she planned to write a guidebook for fellow pacifists. Perhaps she should title it, "How to Successfully Avoid the Truly Determined Sociopath." But she had to deal with Collins, first.

She left a message at the police station for Futura, alerting him to Collins's call. To be certain it was Collins, Page called Rita in the morning to confirm that Rita had not called her the night before, and that Tom was not in the hospital. She hoped that Collins would not start targeting her friends. The crime psychologist she had seen in order to cope with her loss of body parts said that Collins would only be interested in her friends to the extent that he could use them to get to her. So far, the psychologist had been right.

Page checked her car in the apartment garage before she left for work. She had the car made bullet-proof and put in the monitoring system before realizing that Collins never shot her unless she could see him pull the trigger. But it made her feel as if she was doing something to defend herself. The car had one-way reflective glass, too: no one could see in, and if it was too sunny, the glass created a bright sheen, making it too bright to look at comfortably.

She put on the protective vest under her clothes. It was too hot to wear on summer afternoons, but on a cool summer morning, such as this one, it was comfortable enough. It only covered her torso, and a bullet fired close enough with a high-powered gun could get through, but it afforded some protection.

Before she drove away from the garage, her eye scanned the street. She often wondered if Collins regretted shooting her eye out, since the scanner could spot him in a crowd, even at a distance. It was partly because of the eye that he had to work harder to get her in his targeting sight now. In fact, the average time between shootings was becoming longer. Her goal was to make that interval infinitely long. Futura often said that Collins was so heavily involved in the underworld that someone ought to kill him one day, but she was not about to stake her life on that possibility.

She got to work without incident. Collins had not yet tried to breach the security system there. She got home safely afterwards, and for two days after that. She was in her garage, unloading groceries from her car to her pushcart, when her artificial ear picked up the sound of metal grating against metal. Cautiously, she peered around the door. The sound came from the direction of the apartment building. She suspected Collins was around the corner, waiting for her to come out laden with the heavy bags.

He had gotten her that way before; this was why she had bought the pushcart. She went back into the car, dialed the emergency number on her car phone, and explained the situation. She knew the police car was approaching when, from behind the shelter of the garage, she saw Collins run to his car. The police gave chase; she took the groceries into her apartment.

The next time she saw him, he was hiding behind a glare-glass partition at a sidewalk automatic teller station. He seemed unaware that her eye could spot him through it. The glass would prevent a bullet from reaching her—he would have to step out of the station to shoot her. She walked toward it, as if to go past it, but as she reached the edge, her artificial arm snaked in and grabbed the gun. She jerked back; the gun came loose. She tossed it through a storm sewer grate. Collins, apparently in shock, was still there as she turned back to him and grabbed him by the collar, intending to march him to the nearest emergency box and call the police. He struggled violently as she dragged him along; the artificial hand gripped the shirt more tightly. With a savage twist, he lunged forward. The shirt tore loose. She was left holding a large scrap of cloth while he ran, tattered rags on his chest and back. The pedestrians, used to seeing murders in the streets regularly, stared briefly at the strange nonviolent scene and went about their business.

Two weeks and one more failed attempt later, Page was still alive and unshot. Futura came around her workplace and told her that he had won the current pool; the dates had run out. They had started another pool in the office, he said, extending through the next month.

One day, as she stepped out of the building where she worked, something fell on top of her, knocking her down. She looked up and saw that some empty scaffolding had collapsed, trapping her left leg. Collins appeared, running, from behind a corner. Her eye saw every freckle in his face, measured his frame, counted the teeth in his grin.

"Got you again, Page!" he said triumphantly, and shot.

She twisted and put her hand up, as if it would shield her, but the impact hit her back, on the left lower side, below the bullet-proof vest. Collins sprinted off. She turned and used her artificial arm to move aside the debris that had fallen on her. Her artificial leg ignored the trauma of the rest of her body, and hoisted her to her feet. Ignoring the rivulet of liquid running down her back, she stumbled to the nearest police box and pushed the medical emergency button. She slumped to the sidewalk and managed to stay awake long enough to see the ambulance park beside her.

"You awake, or is that just your eye scanning the room?"

She came to her senses and focused on Futura standing above the bed. "I'm awake," she said groggily.

He hefted another dollop of Potato Snax to his mouth. "I don't know whether to congratulate you on your new kidney or go to the funeral for the old one. What do you think?"

"Don't know."

"What now?"

"I'll think about it."

It was a Thursday. Page checked the street before leaving the indoor part of an indoor/outdoor restaurant. There, sitting at an outdoor table, eating, was Collins. He was facing away from her; he did not seem to know she was there. Or did he? Perhaps she could take him by surprise for once. He might just be shamming, waiting for her to get in range to shoot her again, but then again, he might just be eating lunch. Whichever was the case, it was time for her to take the initiative. She was tired enough of being victimized to accept the risk.

She walked cautiously until she was just behind him. He turned, and with a look of genuine surprise, dropped his fork. He twisted in his seat and began to rise. She slammed him back into his chair. "Time for another talk," she said, easing herself into the chair beside him, keeping an eye on his right hand, his gun hand, which clutched the edge of the table.

"There's nothing to say," he sneered. "I'm not joining your League, and I'm not quitting on you, either. You're a thonk. The world don't need no more thonks."

"I know. You're so obsessed with not being a coward, that you have to keep shooting me to prove to yourself that you're not the coward you really think you are."

He banged the table with his fist and stood over her. "You shut up! I'm not a thonk! Only little cockroaches like you are thonks!"

She stared up at him coolly, as he sat again, her eye giving her brain the information that he was six-foot-one, 197 pounds, 20 years old. The blond hair was straight, unruly, and had a cowlick in the back. His shoulders were slightly stooped, and he was double-jointed. She was not surprised by his anger; her psychologist had predicted he would react that way if she said that. "You'll be relieved to know," she added, flexing her artificial arm under the table, "that I'm not here to try to talk you into not shooting me this time. I know now that no one can stop you but yourself."

He smiled mockingly. "And I ain't going to stop myself."

"I don't expect that, either. What I do expect is that sometime, soon, you're going to make a mistake. Your luck is going to run out. And I'm not going to sit idly by anymore waiting for you. From now on, you had better watch for me."

"And just what are you going to do?"

"Figure it out."

He looked up and leered. "That's supposed to scare me?"

"No, I'm just telling you: for my own satisfaction, not yours." She stood. "Bye, now."

When she was at the street corner, he stood and aimed his gun at her. "Got you again, Page!"

She looked on calmly as the gun clicked. Holding up the ammunition clip, she said, "Wonderful what cybernetics can do nowadays, isn't it?"

The passersby looked on curiously at the absurd scene. She went back, unscathed, to the TV station.

Collins left her alone for a month after that. Futura won the pool again; it had never been so long between attacks before. As the time lengthened, Page kept up her state of alertness until it became instinct. Futura told her that although they knew Collins was still in town, and the warrant for his arrest was still outstanding, the department was putting her case on the back burner. The lieutenant still came around work every once in a while, to check if she had seen Collins lately, but he came by less frequently than before.

She began to catch glimpses of Collins, when she was on the street, out shopping, coming back from work. She avoided him when he was far off, but when he was closer, she would circle around behind him and disarm him. If he was trying to intimidate her by showing his face and doing nothing, she could do the same. She kept Futura informed of each incident. He told her that the office had started another pool.

She spotted Collins again after a long day at work. He was looking away as she came out, apparently bored with waiting for her. She went inside again, came out the back entrance, and lifted his gun from behind, tossing it, as usual, into a storm grate.

He swung around with a roar, barbed metal shaft in his hand. Her cybernetic arm blocked it almost without her conscious thought, then twisted around and folded it as if it were a cardboard tube. He pulled out a sling; she tripped him with her artificial leg and the missile flew above her head. She bent down to pick out a bulge at his waist; he pressed the nozzle of a mini-spear shaft gun to her left breast. "This is the end, Page," he said, and fired.

The ricochet off her implant threw her backwards. She landed on her buttocks. She sat there, stunned, seeing that the projectile had bounced back to Collins, catching him under the chin. The other end of the shaft protruded from the top of his head.

Futura was the first policeman to respond to her call. He ran up, gun drawn, took a look at Collins, and put the weapon back in his holster. "Looks like I've won the final pool," he said, indicating the body with a nod.

"He did shoot me," she said.

He waved her statement away. "Nah, it only counts if he injures you."

She peeked inside her blouse to be sure that nothing was damaged, then turned back to the corpse. "He must have forgotten that he had shot me there before," said Page. "It was some time ago, relatively speaking."

"Or else he didn't know that all your implants were armored and enhanced." She turned to him aghast; he added, "Oh. Didn't I tell you that? Authorized by the city precinct. The papers are in your medical files, somewhere."

She shook her head, but smiled.

"Ah, listen, in this business, we need all the living pacifists we can get." Two beat cops ran up; Futura nodded at the corpse. "Why don't you two take charge here; I'll be at the station later to write up a report." He turned to Page. "How about dinner in the meantime? I've got to blow my winnings somehow."

This One Time

Allira Elhalyn-Alton stood in the doorway of her home, watching the riders pass through the gate. It had been only a few hours since the messenger had come. To her husband, Domenic-Lewis, it was the word he'd been waiting for. Baldric Kadarin's raids were taking a large toll—-those not killed outright died a slower death, starved or malnourished, for Baldric took food as well as lives. The previous year's growing season had been poor; this one's did not look more promising. Lord Alton had assembled guardsmen under his command at Armida and sent out scouts to bring back word when Baldric again came across the Kilghard Hills. At last, the message came. Leaving a few of the younger men behind, Domenic now rode out, determined that this raid would be Baldric's last.

"Why must we always stay behind?" remarked Allira's eldest, who stood beside her. Allira gave a resigned shrug in answer as she turned to go inside. She always felt she should have named this daughter Echo, not Bruna. Even before Bruna developed laran, it seemed she was able to speak Allira's mind before Allira spoke it herself.

"Lady Alton?" said a voice behind her as she stepped onto the threshold.

"Yes?" she answered, turning back.

Cathal di Asturien stood in front of her, a step down so she could look at him directly. "Lord Alton gave orders to keep a man on watch at all times," he said, "and lock the gates. I would not plan on going out riding until he returns."

Allira nodded. "I doubt, though, if you will have anything to deal with, except boredom. Baldric is too far away to do much harm to us."

"Baldric is not the only bandit in the hills, lady," Cathal replied.

"We've not been bothered by bandits in a long while."

"Nonetheless, Lady...."

Allira waved his objection aside. "I know, I know, your orders."

"Yes, lady," Cathal said, bowing and descending the stairs.

"I should've cut my hair and put on Kennard or Gwynn's clothes," Bruna muttered behind Allira when Cathal was out of earshot.

"Your father allowed us to learn to handle a sword so we could defend ourselves if need be. I doubt if following him is what he had in mind," Allira replied in an ironic undertone.

Bruna crossed her arms and nodded toward the retreating line of riders. "If I were a man, I'd be heir to Alton and would be riding with them."

"And if I were a man, I'd be on the throne in Thendara!" snapped Allira, more forcefully than she had intended. She sighed, reaching out with her arm and hugging Bruna to her side. Bruna, little Echo, why must you always remind me of my own frustrations? Allira sighed, kissed her daughter, and released her. Bruna said nothing, but turned and went into the house.

Allira sat on the couch in front of the hearth, wrapping a blanket around herself and staring into the fire. As a bride, she had come here in the evenings to be by herself; as the years passed, she grew to regard this spot as her own personal sanctuary, where she could think undisturbed after the family and servants were asleep.

What was to become of Bruna? Allira, too, chafed at feminine restrictions, but she loved her family, and she had enjoyed the work she did in the Tower before she married. Bruna seemed to take little interest in either home or laran. Yet these were the only choices available. Domenic was unlikely to tolerate a grown unmarried daughter in the house much longer. Bruna would have to choose the Tower, as Allira had done at her age. What else was there...?

Allira awakened as a door slammed. Tossing the blanket aside and smoothing her wrinkled dress, she went out of the hall to the entryway to investigate.

"...all the men you can! Hurry," finished Cathal as he clapped the other guardsman on the shoulder. The man, his back to Allira, nodded and left quickly.

"What is it?" asked Allira calmly.

"Men coming down from the heights, Lady Alton," Cathal said urgently. "I told Lorenz to wake the servants and gather the men. The women and children will have to get to somewhere safe."

"Bandits?"

"I don't know, lady, but it's best to be safe. They aren't coming by the road, and they seem to be taking some pains to avoid being seen, though they're doing a clumsy job of it."

"We have a cellar with a strong lock on the inside," Allira volunteered. "It's next to the kitchen. I'll get the children."

Not waiting for an acknowledgement, Allira ran upstairs, jerked open the first door, and went to the nurse's bed, shaking her awake. "Charlena, wake up all the children and get them downstairs to the herb room—now. There are men coming this way. I'll get the baby."

Charlena stared wide-eyed for a moment, then nodded, getting out of bed and fumbled on a robe.

The door banged against the bedroom wall as Allira entered, waking Linnea. She was there where Allira left her, in a crib by the bed. Startled by the noise, Linnea screamed loudly until Allira picked her up. As usual in the morning, Linnea was wet, so Allira wrapped the oilcloth around Linnea's waist and set her on the bed. Allira grabbed her hard leather jacket and pants, slipping on the pants under her petticoats and tying them. She fastened the jacket over her clothes, then took her sword from the cabinet and buckled it on. Linnea watched her idly, sucking her thumb. Good thing she's weaned, Allira thought. She picked Linnea up, oilcloth and all, grabbed a handful of diapers, and headed for the hallway.

"Here, Charlena, take the baby." She handed over Linnea and the diapers, and led the way down to the cellar, followed by a band of sleepy youngsters.

"Mommy, where are we going?"

"What's going on, Mom?"

"Why are you wearing your sword, Mother?"

Allira ignored the questions, heading for the cellar. Bruna strode up, dressed as if for sword practice. She met Allira's eyes for an instant, nodding.

Stopping at the cellar entrance, Allira looked at the servants and their families, already assembling. She spotted the old steward among them. "Eduin?"

The man stepped forward, brushing a stray hair from his face with a gnarled hand. "Yes, my lady?"

"Get everyone into the cellar. Bolt the door and don't come out until someone brings word that it's safe."

"Aren't you coming, my lady?"

"No," Before Allira could add another word, she found herself rocking on her heels, as Kindra and some of the other children pushed against her, clinging to her skirts.

"I don't want to go down there, Mommy. I wanna stay here with you," Kindra said; her brothers and sisters echoed agreement.

Allira disentangled herself gently. "I know you want to stay with Mommy, but you have to go with Charlena and Eduin. You mind them, now!"

Eduin reached down and picked Kindra up. "How'd you like old Eduin to tell you about the time he outsmarted an old banshee?" he said, carrying her down the stairs.

"You never met an old banshee," Kindra said skeptically.

"Oh, yes, I did," said Eduin, turning and winking at Allira as he disappeared, every child in the household in tow.

As the last of the crowd went down the steps, Cathal came around the corner. He started when he saw Allira and Bruna armed and dressed, but continued toward them. "You ought to go down there, too, Lady Alton, Lady Bruna."

"How many men do you have, Cathal?"

"Nine, Lady Alton. Lord Alton took almost everyone who could handle a sword."

"How many are heading this way?"

"About a dozen, I'd say. Hard to tell in the dark, lady."

"With Bruna and me, you'll have eleven, which should even the odds somewhat."

"Yes, lady. But—have you ever killed a man, lady?"

"No. Have you?"

Cathal bit his lip. "I've been in the Guards ten years now, lady," he said simply.

"I've had thirty-six years of training, in case of rape or ambush. I've never had to use what I've learned, but I'm at least as skilled as some of the men you have with you." She turned to Eduin, who had come back up the stairs and was standing by the doorway. "Get inside and lock the door. We'll come for you as soon as we can."

"Yes, lady," Eduin said, as he retreated down the steps. The door swung shut, and Allira heard the thud of a bolt being placed.

"What will Lord Alton say if you're killed, Lady?" Cathal pleaded.

"What would he say if the raiders killed all of you for lack of numbers and then decided to burn the house down around the rest of us?" Allira answered, entering the hall. There were seven men clustered around the fireplace. They turned and stared in shock at Allira and Bruna standing at the other end of the hall. Before anyone could say a word, a man burst through the entrance nearest the front of the house.

"They answered my challenge by throwing stones at me! They're scaling the wall now. I've bolted the front door, but there are other ways of getting in."

The men turned to Cathal. "If they've made it that far, we'd better let them come to us," he said.

"What about the ladies?" someone blurted out.

"The ladies will take care of themselves," Bruna said caustically.

Allira caught Bruna's eye and smiled. Bruna's sword was unsheathed and ready. She hadn't bothered with petticoats, as Allira had done, but wore only a leather jacket, leggings, and the sword. Though the outfit couldn't stop a strong thrust or a direct down-stroke from a heavy longsword, it did provide protection against a casual slash or a glancing cut. Allira fervently hoped the girl wouldn't forget her footwork....

A great bang echoed through the house. The windows rattled with the vibration.

"The doors should hold against anything they might have," volunteered Allira.

"Yes, but they'll try the windows next," said Cathal, as the sound was repeated.

A shattering crash was heard. "Seems as if they've already discovered the windows," Bruna observed, gripping her sword and turning it toward the sound, off in another room.

Yells could be heard outside. The shattering continued, but the pounding at the door stopped.

"Bolt the hall doors!" Cathal ordered. Everyone rushed to the nearest door to slam and secure it. "That will give us a little time, at least," Cathal continued.

"What good is that?" asked Bruna.

"If it's food or money they want, they may just loot the house and leave us alone," said Allira.

"Aye, Lady Bruna, it's always better to avoid a fight if it can be helped. Never lost a man yet in a battle that never started."

Everyone was silent while footsteps could be heard tramping through other rooms in the house. Allira breathed deeply, trying to control her apprehension. A sensitive telepath, she was picking up the tension from the men in the room, ranging from normal fear to near panic. Domenic had told her this was usual for people anticipating a fight, and that he often picked up these feelings himself. Knowing this, though, was proving to be of little comfort to Allira. She was feeling ill, but she shook it off. For one time, even if it was only this one time, she was not going to be pushed aside, protected. She was going to be responsible for her own safety, fully aware of the dangers and the consequences.

The seconds dragged on. Allira began to itch in hard-to-reach places. She heard floorboards creak as the footsteps came closer to the hall.

The door beside Allira split suddenly under an axe blow, flying open with a bang. Allira stepped clear as a man stood at the threshold, pointed a sword at her, and said, "There's the sorceress!"

Allira turned, swept her sword left and found herself engaged with another of the invaders. She quickly assumed an attack position as the man hacked savagely at her. She parried the blow easily and tapped the man lightly on the shoulder, as she did every day to her opponents in sword practice. Surprised to find Allira defending herself so effectively, the man paused for an instant. Embarrassed and startled at using practice techniques against someone who might really kill her, Allira also hesitated—long enough for the man to recover and slice at her ferociously. Allira, bringing all her skill to bear, blocked him at every move. Just as she was beginning to see weakness in his defense, she felt something brush her jacket. Looking down briefly she saw to her horror that there was a sword against her, held by still another man. Allira jumped back; she intended to note as she did so, whether or not the blade had blood on it, but she slipped on something and fell to the floor.

Not looking down, but keeping an eye on the intruders as others stepped in to defend against them, she scrambled to her feet again, planting herself on a firm, dry spot. All the men and Bruna were now occupied; Allira chose the first person fighting more than one man and split the opposition. Her body, she was pleased to notice, moved instinctively, correctly, leaving her mind free to plan future moves. Slowly, she and her new opponent moved away from the main body, both battling aggressively. Time was lost to her until she found an opening for a balestra and used it, making a swift thrust through the heart. Seconds after the man hit the floor, two guardsmen rushed up, hovering over the body.

"He's dead, lady," one of them said, needlessly.

Allira looked from the dead man to her sword and back again.

Then she turned, slowly, surveying the room and counting heads. Seven were standing, all of them recognizable as the original force guarding the hall. Bruna was among them.

"Are you hurt, Mother?" she called from across the room.

"No," Allira answered, looking down at her clothes. There was blood all over them, as well as on the sword. She walked to the center of the room, trying to avoid the pool that had formed on the floor. As she skirted the periphery, she looked down at the men lying there. She'd tended wounded men before, both at the Tower and at Armida, but she had never seen anything like this. She swallowed hard, fighting off nausea.

"Here, Mother," Bruna said, handing her a long rag. Allira wiped her hands and forehead, then cleaned the blade and sheathed it.

"Lady Alton?" Cathal called, getting her attention.

"Yes?" Allira answered, turning toward him.

"Could you take care of Caradoc here? He's hurt."

Allira walked over and looked at the youth, barely sixteen. He moaned softly as she examined him as gently as possible. Determining that he was not beyond aid, she began to rise to get her medical kit, only to find Bruna tapping her arm with it. Allira nodded, accepting it, and knelt again to attend the youth. When she finished with him she turned to the other men. So absorbed was she with her task that she did not notice that no one had spoken to her until she was binding the arm of the last wounded man.

"Lady Alton?" the man asked weakly. He was one of the invaders, not much older than Cathal; what was left of his shirt was faded and threadbare.

Allira nodded. "Yes," she acknowledged kindly, continuing the bandaging.

"You are—not as Baldric described you," he observed.

"Oh?" Allira inquired curiously.

"He said you were an evil sorceress, sending demons to blight the land with the power of your starstone."

Allira put a hand lightly on the man's forehead. It was hot to the touch. She ripped a clean rag free from the bandages and dipped it in a bowl of water nearby, wringing it out. "A matrix is a telepathic amplifier, nothing more," she said softly as she worked. "At the Tower I learned to use telepathy, not to conjure demons." She placed the cloth gently on the man's head.

Cathal stepped up behind Allira, looking down sharply at the stranger. "If you ask me, it is Baldric who is the demon, raiding our lands, robbing us of food, killing our people."

The man looked up at Cathal. "No, Baldric is a good man. He brought us food. My children, my wife...starving until Baldric came. He killed only when necessary...only when they refused to share...."

"He was refused because there is no food to spare, man! We're starving too!"

"But we have no food left! Our stores are gone...our crops... hardly out of the ground...game is scarce. Baldric said the Lady Alton...." The man turned his head away and blinked wearily. The cloth slipped off; Allira caught it and replaced it.

"Watch what you say about the Lady Alton!" Cathal warned.

Allira sighed. "Baldric has long had a grudge against the Altons. He was driven out of the Guards in disgrace for wounding an officer. You have been used, my friend."

The man shook his head slightly and closed his eyes. Allira stood up stiffly. Cathal caught her arm, helping her to her feet.

"You look very pale, lady," he said. When Allira did not reply, he added, "Perhaps you should rest now, lady."

Allira stretched; a sharp pain rippled across her left side. Placing a hand over her ribs and breathing shallowly, she felt the pain ease.

"What's wrong, Mother?" Bruna said, striding up beside Allira and taking her other arm.

"I don't know; I didn't notice any pain there before...."

"Where, Mother?"

"Left side," she said, looking across the hall. "What happened to all the blood?"

"We cleaned it up while you were tending the men. The dead we carried behind the stables. Cathal set some of the others to digging graves for them."

Allira shook her head sadly. "Poor men."

"They would've killed you, lady," Cathal said.

"I know," Allira said softly. "Bruna," she continued, "tell Eduin to come out now. Move the men you can into the guardroom. If they can't be moved that far, bring in some of the cots and get them off the floor, at least." Allira sagged weakly. Cathal and Bruna helped her to the couch.

"Just have to rest," she said, lying on her right side and closing her eyes.

Allira heard voices. Without opening her eyes, she lay still, deciding that she must have slept. The surface she was on was rough; she must still be on the couch. Feeling too tired to open her eyes for the moment, she listened to the voices.

"That was well done, contacting me by matrix, Bruna," said a familiar voice. "Are you sure you're not hurt?"

"Unscathed, Father," answered Bruna.

"Many of my men do not do as well in their first fight," said Domenic. "Perhaps you should've been a man, too?"

Silence followed. Allira attempted to open her eyes, and found it took more effort than she had anticipated. All that happened at first was a slight flutter of the eyelids. Concentrating more, she was able to open them wide enough to get a view of her immediate surroundings.

Coming slowly in focus in front of her, standing at a right angle to her field of vision, was Gabriel. He was leaning forward, his hands on his knees. With typical eleven-year-old brashness, he blurted out, "Gosh, Mom, you look awful!"

Allira tried to laugh, but all that came out was a weak snort, followed by a pain in her side. She closed her eyes and winced, trying to control her breathing.

"Here, dearest, drink this." Allira tried to raise her head, failed, and felt someone lift her head for her. She recognized the fluid by taste as a standard pain remedy. Someone slipped a pillow under her head.

"We had to take several stitches in your side, but it could be worse—your ribs seem to have stopped the blade from going farther," said Domenic reassuringly. "You'll have a scar, though."

Allira managed a weak smile. "The babies?" she murmured.

"All the children are fine. Charlena took the younger ones upstairs by another way and told them Mommy was sleeping. The other ones are here, though—as you no doubt have noticed."

Allira looked away from Domenic and saw her children's faces clustered around the couch, looking at her anxiously.

"Baldric?" she asked.

"We got him," Domenic said. "The poor beggars following him were more starved than our men. Wasn't much of a fight."

"What now?"

Domenic shrugged and knelt next to the couch. "I don't know, Allira. We divided what little food we had, and sent the survivors home. We have little more than they do, and when that runs out...." His voice trailed off.

Allira tried to raise her arm in order to clasp his hand, but managed only to wiggle her fingers. Domenic saw the gesture, took her hand himself, raised it gently and pressed it to his lips.

"The important thing, for now, is that you're safe, dearest," Domenic said, replacing Allira's hand gently at her side. Stroking her hair, he added, "You did very well, they say."

"Bruna?" Allira began weakly.

"She did well, too."

"As well as a man, Father?" teased Bruna, who was standing, looking over the back of the couch.

"Yes," Domenic agreed, reluctantly. For a moment, his face looked strange; Allira wondered if he was having a flash of the foresight that sometimes came to the Altons. At last, he sighed, and said, "You will always do well, daughter." He stood up, facing her.

Bruna smiled. "I intend to, Father," she said confidently.

Allira looked from husband to daughter. Somehow comforted by the expressions she saw there, the feelings that she sensed, she drifted into a peaceful sleep.

Death's Scepter

Regis Hastur, tenerezu of the old Comyn Castle Tower, looked at his younger brother, King Stefan, with kindly concern. Sitting on an upholstered chair opposite him in the visitor's room, Stefan could not meet his eyes. Both strongly laran-gifted, Regis could not help but catch Stefan's thought: *The gods help me, I may have to kill you, bredu.*

Immediately, Stefan lifted his head, so that Regis could see his gray eyes. "I didn't really mean that."

"I know." Regis' gaze strayed to the hilt of Stefan's knife. Emblazoned on it was the Hastur crest with the crown above it. Most thought that was Stefan's own knife; only Stefan and Regis knew that they had exchanged knives, taken the oath of bredin, when Regis was heir-designate of Hastur, and that the crest had been his, then, as crown prince. In a world of kin-strife and blood feud, it was unusual for sons of the same parents to be so close in affection that they would bind themselves to a pledge of mutual protection.

Stefan sighed. "I was beginning to think, at the end of the last council season, that they were starting to accept me at last as the rightful king, not as someone who usurped the throne from my older brother, the one with the Hastur Gift."

"Are you telling me that your healing Belhar Ardais of that mortal wound was not sufficient to impress them? Shall I sit in council again and tell them once more I forfeited the crown of my own free will?"

Stefan shook his head. "It is no use, bredu. Any demonstration of laran skill seems to satisfy them only as long as the memory is fresh. When that begins to fade, it pales against the stories of grandfather Rafael IV and the spell sword, or great-great-grandfather Carolin of Hali and his confiscation of so many wild matrixes when he enforced the Compact, or our more distant ancestors wielding the laran weapons in the Hastur rebellion. I tell you, without the

Hastur Gift, I think sometimes I could impress them only if I passed the two veils at Hali and took up the Sword of Aldones myself!"

Regis smiled. "I have to remind you, bredu." he said softly, "that to manage the Sword of Aldones you would have to have the Hastur Gift."

Stefan nodded. "I have had thoughts, on occasion, of going to Castle Hastur for the Sword of Hastur, except unless an affair involves the honor of the Hasturs, I would be known henceforth as Stefan One-hand."

"Perhaps I should look into the matter to see if the honor of the Hasturs is at stake on questions of the succession."

"Would that it was!"

Regis thought for a moment. "The council season is just beginning...what is it this time? Are the independent fiefdoms putting up a fight again?"

"No, at least, not at present. It's beginning to look like we may eventually be a kingdom of Seven Domains instead of many little territories. Lord Serrais managed to settle with a few more on his borders during the winter. In fact, it's the Leyniers' and Lanarts' struggle for the Alton domain that's the biggest threat at the moment, but for now they're behaving themselves."

"Then it must be the Compact."

Stefan settled back in his chair. "Sometimes I wonder if great-great-grandfather Carolin did us a favor. On one hand, it's clear that the large matrix weapons are forbidden under the Compact, which is good...and everyone can agree that swords and knives are allowable. But there are a lot of cases in between, like last season when we argued whether longbows were allowable. And what did Callista of Arilinn bring up the first day of council season but the question of whether the Compact allowed healing outside a Tower."

"What could have made her think of that?"

"She challenged my competence to judge such a matter. I, who worked in a Tower six years prior to Father's death."

"You could have been tenerezu, if you hadn't been crowned, and she well knows it."

"...and then, it started all over again. Council split, not on the merits of the issue, but by who in council considers me to be the rightful king and who considers me a usurper."

"You know I will help you in any way I can, majesty."

"I know. I know." He rose from the chair. "In truth, I didn't come for advice, but for a sympathetic listener. Thank you, bredu."

Regis followed him to the door. As he walked away, Regis again sensed the anguished thought: *Will I have to kill you, bredu, in order to keep my throne?*

Regis plodded down the hallway, to the room where the matrix screen was. The keeper of the second circle, Gabriela Lanart, would come soon. They would bring Alastair Aillard through to be the new Keeper of the first circle of the new Tower at Comyn Castle. Gabriela had the Alton Gift; she was one of the growing number of women who served as Keepers in the Towers. One day, Regis suspected, most Keepers would be women. For one thing, it had been found that women had more positive energon flows—and they could hold them longer; for another, it was one of the few occupations outside the home open to women.

Regis smiled to himself. Just as there were few occupations open to the eldest son of the Hastur king, he thought.

He leaned back against the wall, smoothing his red mustache. At thirty-two, he thought that he had made the correct moral choice. He did not have the skill to rule, did not have the instinct to know when to leave things alone and when to assert authority, as his brother had. Regis was convinced that no other king could have ruled five years with the contention in Comyn Council, without the extraordinary political acumen that Stefan had. Then again, if Regis had been crowned, there would not be as much friction as now. It had briefly occurred to him that he might have done as well if he had been crowned, naming Stefan his chief adviser. Many rulers before had managed in a similar manner. But to Regis, it seemed right that those who did the work should have the credit; he thought it only fair that if his brother would rule in fact, he should rule in name, as well.

Besides, Regis found, when sent for a few years of training in the Towers, that this was the life he was born to: he enjoyed it, and he was good at it, particularly after his father had awakened the Hastur Gift in him. Stefan had enjoyed it, too, even after Father had failed to awaken the Gift in him, but Stefan seemed to like any task he was good at, whether hawking, training cadets, monitoring matrixes, making babies, or speaking in council.

Regis stood when Gabriela entered the room. Like many Comyn women, she was tall and thin, with bright red hair. Mutual recognition required only a moment for a thought to pass between them.

Gabriela motioned to the screen. "Shall we?"

Within minutes, Alastair Aillard stood between them, brushing off his robe. "I tell you," he said, "no matter how many times I go through these screens it's always unsettling. I check my fingers and toes to see if they're still there." He held up his hands. "Good. Six each. I'll count my toes when I'm settled in the old Tower. I presume my baggage preceded me?"

Gabriela smiled at him. "It arrived yesterday. Don't worry."

"Speaking of worry, old friend," Alastair brushed the back of Regis' hand with a fingertip, an intimate greeting among telepaths, "I have a warning for that brother of yours. Denita Elhalyn came back from wintering at the castle and told me her scruffy little brother, Valentine, is plotting something. He was very secretive about it, especially around his Tower-trained big sister, but she's certain that it's not a trifle. She says he mutters things such as if the Hastur of Hasturs won't put the right man on the throne, the Hasturs of Elhalyn will."

Gabriela inhaled sharply as Alastair was speaking. When he finished, she said, "I saw my cousin Cyril Leynier yesterday. He said he was worried that his friend Valentine was late for the council session. I didn't think much of it at the time, but...."

Regis nodded. Cyril and Valentine were younger relations of their domain lords, grasping for attention by making nuisances of themselves last season. They were prominent in Stefan's reports last year when he unburdened his problems with Regis. "I'll give him the message."

"Good," said Alastair.

"I'll send for someone to escort you to your rooms," said Regis. "Since there is nothing on our schedules for tonight, I hope you'll come back here and dine with Gabriela and me."

"Delighted."

After Alastair was gone, Regis went to his room. There, using his individual matrix, he contacted Stefan.

"Cyril and Valentine," mused Stefan. "No, that's not a surprise. Whatever they've planned, if it appears to the others that it has a chance of working, every Comyn in the council who opposes me will join them to supplant me, weak as the Elhalyn claim to the throne might be. You have no idea exactly what they're up to?"

"None."

There was a pause. "Thank you, bredu. I will handle it."

"If there is some way I can help...."

"I know."

Contact was broken. Regis rewrapped his matrix in its insulating fabric and let it fall back to his throat. Although he often offered to help Stefan, Stefan rarely took him up on his offers. Not that he could blame Stefan: in political matters, Regis had made embarrassing mistakes, as heir-designate, that Stefan had helped him set right again. Not for the first time, Regis wondered if the best solution all around might be for him to take his own life. What had stopped him before was the thought that Stefan might be accused of killing him and making it look like suicide, which could make matters even worse. On the other hand, if the thought crossed Stefan's mind, to kill him, maybe it would make matters better. Then again, maybe he should just get lost. He could easily teleport to a remote area and travel by foot to one of those isolated communities near the Wall Around the World. In searching for unmonitored matrixes following the Ages of Chaos, the Towers had records of known or suspected locations. But could he get far enough away so that the Towers or Domains would never find him? He wasn't sure.

Dinner was in a small room next to Gabriela's. After the meal, each of them sat back sipping hot spiced cider. Regis looked over to Alastair, who, in the dim light of the room, seemed more like a wood spirit then a man. His red hair was going gray at the temples; his craggy face was furrowed by a network of wrinkles. He was a head shorter than Regis, and many years older.

"You look far more worn than I, my friend," said Alastair to Regis as if guessing Regis' thoughts. "Been stalking the wild matrix again?"

Gabriela groaned. "After last year, I don't want to see another one."

"Nor I," said Alastair. "But I fear we shall. Our ancestors seem to have had more matrix weapons than there are leaves on the trees in the forest. Varzil the Good and his colleagues gathered up all the large ones, very many of them. In the years since then, we've found many more. But ever since I was a lad in the towers, it seems that every summer, a farmer finds another while tilling a field or a pair of friends finds one while fording a stream. A guardsman found one while sheltering on the road in a woodsman's house—the family had no laran, and they thought it a pretty trinket for their fireplace mantel. I daresay we'll find more before we're through."

"At that rate, we'll go on finding them for generations untold!" said Gabriela.

Alastair smiled. "Even the leaves of the forest aren't limitless. No, I think finds will become ever more rare until we find all those not deeply hidden. In my time, most discoveries have not been very powerful matrixes. Well-insulated, high-powered ones may escape notice a few more generations, but I think it will not be long before we find all those of consequence."

"Just the same, I could stand one or two more years of quiet before finding another one," said Gabriela.

Alastair held out his glass in Regis' direction. "As long as we have friend Hastur, here, I think we need not worry. He's a powerful matrix all in himself. And enjoys it, too, don't you, my friend?"

Regis recalled the fear and exhilaration he felt as he acted as focus for the Tower circle. It was not the first time he had made use of the Hastur Gift, but it was the first time he had faced so deadly a challenge. Even now, he still did not know which had been greater: the thrill of accomplishment, or the dread that he might fail, be burned to a cinder, or thrust out of the world forever.

"It is good for your brother that no one outside the Tower saw you then," said Alastair. "The Hastur glamour was about you for certain. The common folk, even some of the Comyn, are superstitious still—expecting their king to display incredible powers."

* * *

It was a quiet evening, though this was ordinarily the time the Towers were at work. Probably Neskaya and Arilinn were, Regis thought as he looked out the window of his room. Tonight, however, in deference to Alastair's arrival, and because of no pressing needs in their vicinity, the two Towers of Comyn Castle were at rest. Drizzle fell outside; through it Regis could see lights in the Hastur suite. Stefan playing with the children before bedtime, or Stefan wondering what to do about Cyril and Valentine? Probably both, guessed Regis, knowing his brother.

Turning, he saw the barracks area and two adjoining courtyards. Beyond them, the night watch patrolled the walls. Over the wall, Regis could see lights from the city. He wondered what the people thought of Stefan. Were they split in opinion, like the Comyn were? He regretted he did not know. Regis rarely left the Tower, rarely stepped outdoors, except when Tower work demanded it. He preferred living that way. Was he wrong to have done so?

Regis woke gasping, hand at his throat. No one had taken the insulation off his matrix and touched it, though it felt as if someone had. He slipped out of bed, reaching for...not the red robes of a tenerezu, or the blue of a matrix technician, but the blue embroidered shirt which matched his eyes, the black pants with the silver trim, black leather boots, silver-gray cloak lined with blue—the Hastur colors.

Slowly, softly, he went down the stairs. No other in the tower was awake. Was it a false alarm, or something attuned only to his laran? In either case, it was directional, and he was going in the right direction. Out the door, through a gallery...Regis knew the castle from boyhood, but it had been some years since he had explored it extensively. And now, a door to the courtyard. Hearing voices, Regis kept close to a wall in the shadows. The drizzle had stopped. It must be near dawn, he thought. As the clouds broke, the light of two moons outlined five figures, and glinted off an object. It looked like a gold-plated rod.

"I found it last autumn, when I camped in the ruins of an old castle," said one of the figures.

"How does it work, Valentine? Have you tried it?" said another.

"Yes. You take the insulation off, point it at something, concentrate, and it kills whatever you aimed at. I brought down a wild chervine that way."

Regis already had his matrix out, contacting Alastair, then Gabriela. They could alert others.

Almost there, said Gabriela in his mind. *I heard you walk past my bedroom.*

"Let's try it on something," whispered a voice in the courtyard. "There's a bird perched on a wall, over there."

"No!" said Regis, stepping forward.

He heard the sounds of swords being drawn. "Who goes there?" shouted a figure.

"Regis-Mikhail Hastur of Hastur!"

"Vai dom," said Valentine. He held out the rod. "Take this and assume your rightful place among the Comyn."

At first Regis was startled. Did this mean Valentine's motive wasn't to try to claim the throne for himself or his lord? Then, without stopping to think how Valentine might react, Regis answered, "I will not rebel against the rightful king." He sensed someone step behind him. *Gabriela,* she whispered in his mind.

Valentine pulled the rod back. "If you will not, we will!"

"Fool!" said Regis. "You'll destroy yourself."

He ran forward to snatch at the rod, but Valentine stepped back. His companions blocked the way. Regis felt, rather than saw, Valentine take the insulation off the rod. Instantly, there was enough light to see by.

"Hey!" said Valentine. "It didn't act this way before!"

"Drop it!" said Regis. He and Gabriela linked to oppose the power coming from the artifact. Valentine screamed and let go, but it was too late—the thing was activated. When his gift was in use, Regis' awareness was limited to telepathic forces. He knew Valentine's companions had fled only because of low, receding thought impressions. The thing's power had burst forth like a column of flame. Regis shielded himself and Gabriela, then reached out to contain the alien force. He succeeded in preventing it from spreading, but to force it into quiescence, he needed more help. The thing was bleeding reserves from him, from them.

Then...ah! a solid, steady strength joined them, one they could lean against, one that stood fast: Alastair, probably. At the center of the resistance, Regis coordinated the forces, using the additional energy to quench the fire, insulate the matrix, bring it under control.

It was done. Regis found himself kneeling on the flagstones, breathing heavily. Looking up, he saw the red light of dawn spread rapidly across the sky above the castle walls. Within the courtyard stood a large crowd. All of the cadets in the barracks must have come out, and not a few of the Comyn lords and heirs. A fading blue glow reflected off their faces.

Now, Regis thought dejectedly, it will be harder than ever to convince them to accept Stefan as the rightful king. Again, Regis looked at the awe-struck expressions, trying to think of a way to salvage the situation. But this time he noticed they were not looking directly at him, but to his right. Tilting his head upward, he saw Stefan standing above him, holding the rod, wrapping insulation around the matrix at its end. The air around him still shimmered with a pale blue light. Regis was still on his knees. Hearing the sounds of movement, he turned to see the assembly kneel by ones and twos, then as a group.

By the time Stefan had finished shielding the matrix, the glimmer had vanished. He turned to the assembly. "Lord Alton, take charge of your cadets."

He rose. "Yes, majesty." There was not a thimbleful of disrespect in his tones.

As the cadets filed out, Lord Elhalyn walked forward to cover a body with his cloak.

"I grieve for your loss, Lord Elhalyn," said Stefan.

He nodded. "If I'd known he'd had a wild matrix, I would have told Denita to alert the Towers immediately."

While Elhalyn signaled his men to take the body away, Stefan reached down. "Are you all right, bredu?" he asked, hoisting Regis to his feet.

"Yes. Was that you? Thank you."

Stefan smiled. "Didn't think I had it in me, bredu?"

"On the contrary," said Regis. "But I didn't know you were nearby."

Stefan shrugged. "I was drawn somehow. I don't know how."

"Drawn through Regis' distress, perhaps," said Gabriela. Regis turned to see her standing behind him. She was dressed in a long red robe and covered by a long red veil.

At that moment, Alastair walked up. Seeing Stefan, he bowed. "Majesty."

Stefan nodded.

"I think, Majesty," said Alastair, "that you have given a demonstration of the powers of a Hastur king that few will forget."

"I hope so," said Stefan. "In the meantime, as senior tenerezu of the towers of Comyn Castle, will you take charge of this weapon?"

"Gladly, Majesty," said Alastair. Regis caught the additional thought: *the king is indeed as strong as a tenerezu.*

Stefan smiled at Alastair, then glanced at Regis. Regis nodded; he knew how it might look if Stefan handed the artifact to him. Alastair and Gabriela bowed and exited, leaving Stefan and Regis to themselves.

"Council is in session after breakfast," said Stefan. He took a long deep breath. "I'm weary, but I think I'll last the day without a nap." He touched the back of Regis' hand with a fingertip in farewell. "Long life to you, bredu." He walked back to the castle.

...and to you, thought Regis.

Mind-eater

Domenic MacAran tried to shake off the sense of foreboding that increased with each dogged step up the ancient stone stairs. A nedestro son of the Altons, he had the Alton Gift, but his mother had been a nedestro daughter of the Aldarans, so that Domenic had also had occasional flashes of insight about the future. It was this sense that nagged him now. But he could not go back: the tower where he had been under-Keeper was now in ruins, destroyed in the lowland wars that raged in the Domains. No, the only cure for his war-weariness was to get away, go as far into the Hellers as he could, find a village so isolated that the Domains were only a rumor, and laran-weapons a fairy tale. He'd been raised by a family of modest means; he could earn a living as a herdsman or a carpenter or stonemason. He'd served in the Guards: he might earn a living as a body-guard, if one of the mountain lords in this area could support one. Wherever he settled, he must do it quickly—winter was fast approaching, and he could not wander the Hellers, alone, in the inevitable storms and blizzards that would come.

In the meantime, there were the stairs. They had appeared at the end of an overgrown dirt track, the rock splintered by years of frost, but not worn smooth by use. Weeds sprouted from the cracks. He had thought it a natural rock incline until he saw a spot where two stone slabs had been fitted together. He took his matrix, the starstone around his neck, and examined it more closely. The foundation showed no mortar or mark of any tool. The stairs bad been laid by matrix workers, long, long ago. To be sure that there was no existing Tower, he had gone into the overworld, where any Tower would leave its mark. There was none, but his sense of impending danger had begun at that moment.

He reached the top of the stairs. Looking up, he saw night fall, the ragged edges of a dark starry blanket coming toward him, over him, then behind him to the far horizon. Idriel and Liriel had risen, lighting the way.

A stone road appeared in front of him. He came to a village. There was a fountain in the village square. He stopped to drink, and wash, and fill his water bottle. He looked around for a likely place to knock on the door and ask for shelter for the night. Light shone through the shuttered windows of the small stone houses, but his attention was drawn to the dark face of an edifice beyond the village.

No! Leave me alone!

Domenic put his hand on his sword hilt, stood, and turned. No one was there. He had heard no sound. Hand on his matrix, he peered into the overworld. He saw a youth, with the physique of a runner-messenger, sprinting across the gray plain. A youngster with newly-developed laran having a nightmare, Domenic guessed. In that case, if he could find the house, he could offer his assistance as a laranzu to the family. Laran-gifted children in remote areas suffered unless they could teach themselves control or had the milder forms of threshold sickness. But as he turned to the houses, the overworld image was gone. Before putting his matrix away, something about the houses caught his attention. They, too, were matrix-constructed, just as the castle in Thendara had been. Who would waste Tower energy on village houses? And in an area where the nearest Tower was a tenday's ride away?

Clouds obscured the moons. It began to snow. He knocked at the door of a house. Before he could say anything, the woman who answered spotted his starstone, said "Laranzu!" in a startled whisper, and slammed the door in his face. At every other house in the village, it was the same. Domenic sat in the snow powder and wiped his forehead on his sleeve, though he was not sweating. In the lowlands, he had been treated with respect, even awe, but he had never been shunned. In the Domains, even the most ragged beggar might find shelter for the night in the rudest of huts. Why did these villagers refuse him?

Domenic turned back to the edifice. It was larger than the castle in Thendara; had he not seen it earlier by moonlight, he might have mistaken it for a mountain. No light came from any window or door. He might have tried to spend the night in an animal shelter instead, but the smell of straw and hay would stop up his nose. He walked to the castle.

He halted before the wooden double doors. These were in good condition, on their hinges, latched, but not locked. He unfastened the catch and pushed. The door swung open easily, silently. He called inside. Nothing answered. With his matrix, he kindled a cold blue light in his hand. Domenic stepped in, closing the door behind him.

He stood in an entry hall. In front of him and to his left was a stone staircase. Beside that was a hallway. To his right, there was another door, presumably leading to a chamber. To his far left, there was an open entryway to a vaulted hall. Holding the light in his hand in front of him, he walked in.

The bare wooden floor was clean. His sensitive nose detected no dust. In the middle of the long wall was a fireplace, taller than he was, with dry wood stacked next to it. He walked up to it, put down his pack and sword, laid fuel on the hearth, and kindled a fire with his matrix. Then, he extinguished the blue light. Hungry from the long day's climb and from the use of his laran, he ate a large meal from the store of food in his travel pack. Spreading his bedroll in front of the hearth, he prepared to sleep.

A hideous scream made him sit up and reach for his sword. Shrill curses echoed in his ears; the vilest language he had heard since leaving the Guards. It echoed in the hallways, reaching his ears in this large room. Then it stopped.

Domenic sat quietly, his heart racing. In his mind he recalled childhood tales of haunted castles and demon-possessed artifacts. But he was a Tower-trained telepath, and he knew such things were not so.

Are they not, little man?

Domenic stood, clutching his sword, and swung around before realizing he had not heard a voice but had, instead, received a telepathic message. "Show yourself!" he called. Although he was small in stature, he had become the best swordsman in the Guards, and when he received a wound serious enough to be sent to a Tower for healing, he became the most skilled telepath there, who would have succeeded the Keeper had he lived to lay down his office. No one mocked Domenic MacAran for his size and went unchallenged.

As if in answer, something ripped at his mind, as if banshee claws were scraping his brain. Domenic put a hand to his face, breathing heavily. After the shock of the attack had passed, he recognized the tearing rapport as a reflection of his own gift. Angrily, he thrust back, putting all his strength in resistance. A cry echoed in his thoughts. The pain stopped, and he fell to his knees.

His first instinct was to flee. A single telepath could not have a range he could not get away from. But there was a snowstorm outside. He would have to go beyond the limits of the village, by that time, he might be dead of the cold. No, whoever it was, whatever it was, he'd have to face it. Here. Now.

Putting his sword down, Domenic sat and took out his matrix to find his opponent. In the overworld, Domenic's image of himself was that of a large, muscular man. Let his opponent see that, if he would! But he saw no opponent. The runner-messenger was there; a woman, tall and silent; an emmasca, huddled and frightened; a clawed crustacean, like the ones from the ocean beyond the Aillard Domain. Dream images, none menacing. His opponent was hiding telepathically, but he—and Domenic sensed his opponent was male—had a physical presence, and that Domenic could find. He took his Keeper's kit of small matrixes and telepathic tools, and his sword, and walked from the hall, leaving his bedroll and the rest of his pack behind.

Domenic had invaded fortresses before. He knew how to search for hidden opponents, knew what precautions to take. Sword in one hand, blue matrix light in the other, he padded up the stairs to the topmost level. The floors were swept, the beds made, but no one was there. He wondered how such a large castle could be kept so clean. It should take an army of servants to maintain such a large building.

He went to the next lower level, and the next. Again there was a shriek, followed by cursing. He crept toward the noise, sword raised. At an intersection of hallways, he looked to the right, then to the left. The dim blue light revealed a bulge in the wall.

"I see you," called Domenic. "Show yourself."

The bulge did not move, but Domenic could hear stressed breathing. Cautiously, he moved forward. A form took shape. It was a large young man, his arms and legs twisted at odd angles. Shakily, the man's thick fingers reached for a matrix at his throat. Not wanting to be taken again by his own Gift, Domenic reached out and overwhelmed the figure's mind. The younger man cried out softly in response to the forced rapport. Domenic saw the image of the runner-messenger and withdrew immediately.

Domenic held the blue light to the figure's face. "I'm sorry," he said. "I thought you were someone else."

The figure turned toward him, tears of pain in his eyes. Again, the fingers reached for the matrix, which, unlike Domenic's, was unshielded.

My name is Ruyvil. I cannot speak clearly, the figure said into Domenic's mind. *I was born with my limbs twisted so.* Putting his hand down, Ruyvil moved away from the wall. He took a couple of steps, dragging one foot, and stopped in front of Domenic.

"I see," said Domenic. "I was looking for another. Is there another man here, a laranzu, perhaps, like myself?"

The round face puckered, the expression pinched, as if in pain. Ruyvil shook his head repeatedly, compulsively. Domenic tried to reach his thoughts, gently, but he was barricaded, and Domenic hadn't the heart to force himself into his mind again.

A shriek made Domenic turn, sword raised. He walked back into the middle of the hallway intersection. He heard a shuffling. Ruyvil walked toward him, one twisted arm extended, as if pleading. Domenic heard a string of curses. A woman came into view. She walked normally, but her head twitched.

A touch on his shoulder made him start. Ruyvil had his other hand on his matrix. *Her name is Mirella. Truly, she is harmless.*

Mirella stopped in front of them. A thick cord ringed her neck. Her matrix, threaded by a strand of spider silk, was tied to that cord. She thrust a trembling hand under the cord to steady it, and touched the matrix with a finger. In his mind, Domenic saw the quiet, still woman he had spotted in the overworld, a contrast to her real self.

A tall figure came from the shadows. Domenic did not hear him coming, did not see him until he came into the view of Domenic's blue hand-light. The emmasca?

"Yes," he said aloud. "I am Gareth. We...."

Mirella, Ruyvil, and Gareth shrieked and crouched, hands to their ears as if shutting out a painful noise. Domenic slammed his mind shut against the effect, but not before he caught the thought of his opponent:

Fool! Do you think you can escape me? All here are under my control!

This was intolerable. Even using his full Alton Gift to shield himself, Domenic could feel something thrumming against his barriers, like a battering ram against a gate. He strode ahead to the nearest door. Any Great House occupied by telepaths had to have a room with a damper. He'd find one if he had to go through every room.

Fortunately, he found one on that floor, probably a small presence-chamber used by the forgotten lord of this castle. He went back to the intersection and hauled Mirella and Gareth, one on each arm, to the room. Then he went back for Ruyvil. He half-dragged, half-carried the young man, but got him there at last. He took one of his matrixes, keyed to his own brain pattern, and locked the door with it. Then he turned on the damper.

The other three telepaths collapsed, moaning. Gareth sat up first. "Thank you," he said.

"Speak quickly," said Domenic. "Our adversary could come up at any moment, break the door, and turn off the damper."

"No," said Gareth, "he cannot do that."

"Of course he can," said Domenic. "The matrix will keep the door locked, but won't keep him from breaking the hinges."

"Gareth is right," said Mirella. She shrieked. "Castimir has no legs. He cannot go anywhere—" She let out a string of loud curses. "—faster than a crawl."

"I read of some of his life in his mind," said Gareth. "He was born of a mother raped in a lowland campaign. She fled to the house of a minor lord and became a servant there. Castimir made a name for himself as a mercenary soldier. He showed nothing but contempt for those who had any physical defect. Somehow he got involved in a blood feud. Knowing his mind, those he fought against drugged him so he could not use his laran, then cut off his legs instead of killing him. When he recovered his strength and his laran, he used his gift to kill those who had disabled him. Then he overwhelmed the mind of a strong man and compelled the man to carry him on his back, away from the lowlands. He forced the man to feed him, clothe him, find him shelter. By the time the strong man climbed the steps to the village here, Castimir had worn his caretaker out. The man died, and Castimir compelled the people of the village to house him here, feed him, clean for him, wait on all his needs, as if he were an overlord here."

"Has anyone tried to kill him?" asked Domenic.

"Those who have..." Mirella whooped. "...have died." She let out a string of curses.

"He can compel people to jump off a cliff, fall into a well...." Gareth shrugged.

"Does he have a matrix? A starstone?" asked Domenic.

"Yes," said Gareth. "He took one from one of the lowlanders he killed and keyed it to himself."

"Damn! If we were only near a Tower," said Domenic.

"We are," said Gareth, "in a way."

Domenic turned to him.

"We are a small village," Gareth said, "but a proud one. Once we were the center of laran-skill in Darkover. We were kin to the chieri, as you can still see in some people, like me. The first telepath circle was in this castle, only underground. Towers were built later, as our knowledge spread to the lowlands and took root there. We are not what we were, but the babes here learn at their parents' knee what a matrix is, what laran is, what to do when it comes upon a body, and how to live with it after. Our skills and knowledge are not now what they are in the lowlands, but it all started here."

"How many telepaths are in the village?"

"We are the strongest," said Gareth, "which is why Castimir keeps us here because can control us more easily."

"That is not..." Mirella let out a string of curses. "...all."

Gareth hung his head, embarrassed.

Mirella explained, pausing when her head twitched, or when she whooped or cursed. "We are not only here because of our...laran. We are here because when Castimir came...and began to control the laran-gifted...the villagers bargained with him.... If he would...take us for himself...they could send their laran-gifted...kin out of his reach."

Domenic nodded. Now he knew why he had been turned away from the houses. The villagers thought he was another Castimir. "But you said he forces the villagers to care for him, too."

"Yes," said Gareth, "that was also part of the bargain. In exchange for leaving their kin alone, they must provide for him. He forces them if they forget."

Domenic sat. After some thought, he said, "You said there was once a telepath circle here?"

"Yes," said Gareth, "but underground, on the lower levels of the castle."

"Have any of you ever been there?"

They looked from one to the other. Gareth said, "No. There's no reason to go there."

Domenic stood. "Show me."

They looked to the door, terrified. Mirella shrieked. Gareth said, "But outside this room, he'll control us again."

"We can't stay here," said Domenic. "For one thing, there's no food. And we must defeat him."

"How?" said Gareth.

"If there was once a Tower circle here, there has to be at least a second-, third-, or fourth-level matrix around. All of us working together, with that sort of screen, should overwhelm him."

"But we know nothing..." Mirella cursed. "...of such sorcery."

"I know," said Domenic. "There is a risk, since there is no monitor for us, and none of you have worked in a Tower circle before. But none of you are new to the use of your laran. I can draw you in and keep you steady. Provided it does not take all night, we should be safe. What do you say?"

They looked from one to the other. Gareth said, "We are agreed, but how to get down to the matrix-chamber without Castimir ripping our minds apart? For he surely shall if he senses what we wish to do."

"Let me try this," said Domenic. "The damper will have thrown him off our scent, so to speak, and when I turn it off, he might not realize immediately where you are. With my Gift, I can overwhelm your minds, and thus protect you with my own resistance. Then I can lead you to the lower levels by the hand. Can you trust me to do this? I can only do it if you are willing."

The others consented. Domenic turned off the damper. One by one, Domenic put their laran under his control. As he worked, he thought that this also would help them work smoothly within the matrix circle, for by the time they reached the lower chambers, at Ruyvil's pace, they should be deeply in rapport and attuned to each other.

Once their minds were protected by his, and his own thoughts barricaded, he linked arms with Mirella on his right, Ruyvil on his left. Gareth took Ruyvil's other arm to steady him. Slowly, slowly, they walked down the hall and descended the stairs. Even barricaded, Domenic could sense Castimir's thoughts searching him out on the surface of his awareness:

Fool! Do you think you can thwart me so?

Domenic ignored his adversary. It was taking a great mental effort to protect them all from Castimir: Domenic could understand how he could keep three telepaths and one village under his sway. But the matrix—and he hoped there was a matrix—would amplify their thoughts at least fourfold.

At last, the four reached the lower regions of the castle. There was a door there, with an ancient matrix lock, still activated. Domenic uncovered his matrix, gathered the other three in his rapport, matched resonances with the lock, and released it. The door swung open.

Domenic led the other three into the room. There was a damper there. He released the three others and turned it on. Then he closed the door. The matrix lock reactivated, making the room secure.

"What now?" asked Mirella. She cursed.

When he had turned the telepathic damper on, a dim glow issued from the ceiling. "We find the matrix," answered Domenic. He strode through the chambers of the underground levels. There was a familiarity about them. He could well believe that there had been telepath circles here, perhaps even the first telepath circles on Darkover.

He found a room with a third-level matrix. He walked around it, examined it, and found it workable. Turning toward the entrance, he saw Mirella, Gareth, and Ruyvil looking on curiously.

"This is where we will work," said Domenic. "Mirella, you sit here; Gareth, here; Ruyvil, here. I will turn the damper off from here. When I sit, we will begin."

"What will..." Mirella cursed. "...happen?"

"We will fight him in the overworld," said Domenic.

"The gray plain?" said Gareth. "But that is illusion."

"It can be," said Domenic. "But the effects can be quite real. Tower battles have been fought in the overworld before. Injuries and deaths to the participants have been recorded."

"Could we die?" said Gareth.

"We could," said Domenic. "But working together, with the help of the matrix, we should have the advantage. If you don't want to do this, I will try it alone with a Tower level matrix or with only one or two of you. If you have the slightest doubt about this, I want you to quit now. There is no disgrace in standing aside in this matter, for anything less than full cooperation from any of you could kill us all, once we begin."

"I will help you." Mirella let out a whoop.

Ruyvil motioned that he wished to join the circle.

"Death would be better than being his tool for the rest of his life," said Gareth.

"Just think with me," said Domenic. "The rapport will be very much like it was when I brought you down here." He sat and turned off the damper. Again, there was a respite—the damper apparently threw Castimir off-balance, temporarily unable to reach his victims. Domenic fell into a tentative rapport with the large matrix, then drew the others in, one by one. Mirella, despite her body twitch, was rock-solid as a telepath. Ruyvil, in contrast to his handicap, was strong and supple. Gareth was energetic and steady. Just as Castimir made contact, Domenic thrust them all into the overworld. Here, Domenic was a tall, muscled warrior fending off Castimir's attack, which was represented in the gray dream-stuff as spears against Domenic's unyielding shield.

That's Castimir, said Ruyvil, whose thoughts were speech in the overworld. The shelled creature.

Peering over his psychic shield, fending off Castimir's barbs, Domenic spotted the shelled crustacean he'd noticed before.

So that was how Castimir pictured himself, thought Domenic. Impregnable and unreachable. But Domenic had been by the sea, and eaten such creatures for dinner. He knew how to break their shells. Keeping up his shield, he altered his dream-shape to that of Zandru at his forge. His companions quickly picked up on the image, and as Domenic grew, towering over Castimir, arms bulging, Ruyvil became a hammer in Domenic's hand, Gareth formed a wall to protect them from Castimir's barbs as Domenic took shape, and Mirella became an anvil that slipped under Castimir's form. Startled by the change in strategy, Castimir had time only to raise his claws in a vain attempt to fend off the hammer as it came down on his shell.

With a gasp, the four telepaths returned to their bodies in the matrix chamber. Domenic quickly checked the overworld with his personal matrix. The Castimir image was gone. There was a mental silence. Domenic reached out for contact with Castimir's mind. Their adversary was either barricaded or dead.

"Is he gone?" asked Gareth.

Ruyvil touched his matrix. *I will not be satisfied until I see his body.*

"Where does he usually stay?" said Domenic. "We could check those rooms."

Gareth led him to a suite in the middle of the castle, on an upper floor. There, lying on a bed, was a legless body. It looked as if he had been crushed.

Gareth leaned against a wall and slid to the floor, exhausted. "It's over."

Mirella came in soon after, leaning on Ruyvil's arm. They looked in on the body and sighed.

"It's over for Castimir," said Domenic, "but I am uneasy about there being a third-level matrix close at hand. If Castimir had known of it, and known how to use it, he would have been all but invincible. Or, worse, if a group of Tower-trained telepaths had descended on you with ill will, this whole castle, and the area here, could have been reduced to rubble."

What is to be done, then? said Ruyvil.

"Stay and guard it against misuse," said Domenic. "Then, too, we can put it to good use—a small circle with even a relatively low-level matrix could do a bit of mining close by, keep the roads in repair, and the summer fires under control. I could teach you, if you wish, or I could teach the laran-gifted in this village, who will probably return when news of Castimir's death reaches their kin here."

We will fare no better anywhere else, said Ruyvil.

"I bear no ill will toward my kin in the village," said Gareth. "They did what they thought best to save themselves."

"I will..." Mirella whooped. "...stay."

Domenic nodded. "Good. We can probably earn our keep through mining alone. I think, after this, the villagers will leave this castle to us. One day, when the Domains stop fighting, we can send to a Tower to have the matrixes here recorded and monitored. Until then, we have our life's work ahead of us."

No one can play the tyrant with us again, said Ruyvil.

"No," agreed Domenic. "Here we can have peace, if we work to keep it." His foresight assured him that it would be so.

The Honor of the Guild

Janna n'ha Cassilde studied the body in front of her carefully. The man should not be dead. There were no marks of violence, no signs of illness. She uncovered the matrix around her neck, hoping her laran would reveal something. It did not. Tucking the rewrapped matrix back into her tunic, she turned, thinking to speak to the deceased's wife. A crowd had silently gathered behind her, in this old, dim shack where the body lay.

Janna ignored the staring eyes. "And you say a Renunciate did this, mestra?" she asked the woman.

"Ay, ay, no mistake. She had her hair sheared off—wore pants, and a sword just as you have." The woman pulled her head scarf closely around her face, obscuring her features.

Janna scratched an ear. The woman's accent was rustic, not the learned casta or the city-dialect of cahuenga she was used to, but she could make out the words. The Renunciate turned back to the body, half-expecting it to rise up behind her, but it was as still and cold as before. "And you say she just looked at him and he fell dead."

"Ay, ay." The words were slower this time, less certain.

"And there was no reason to kill him, you say?"

"Nah, nah, no reason. Just out in the field, minding the crops." The widow glanced nervously from Janna to another man in the room, named Ruyvil, who appeared to be one of the more prominent men in the poor village.

"All Renunciates are crazy, if you ask me," he blurted out. "The Comyn Council should revoke your charter, and marry you all to men who would whip you into shape. The Dry Towners have the right idea—keep the women in chains!"

Janna ignored him. "I am sorry for your loss," she said to the widow. "I, too, have a freemate, and he is very dear to me...."

"A sandal-wearer, no doubt," mumbled Ruyvil.

"If your family needs help with the harvest, I and my Guild-sisters will do what we can."

"Na' thank you, mestra," said the widow, pulling back a little to make it even harder for Janna to see her face. "I ha' three grown sons to help me, two unmarried."

Janna reached out to give the widow a reassuring embrace, but the smaller woman flinched away. Instead, Janna murmured a polite formula and walked out.

Outside, away from the close air of the shack and its many mourners—Janna had no doubt that in such a small town, the whole village must be in there—she inhaled a deep draught of the cool, fresh air. The hamlet was in Ridenow territory, almost equidistant from the Serrais estates, the Alton estates, and the Dry Towns—which was to say, right in the middle of nowhere. Normally, a town this size would not have a Renunciate Guild House, but a modestly wealthy matron of the area had joined the Renunciates in her widowhood, and, being childless, left the Guild a horse ranch, which was now the Guild House and headquarters for the Guild in this area. Besides keeping the other Guilds supplied with mounts, some of the Guild-sisters were midwives to the women in the scattered villages, traveling the area in circuits, checking on clients. There was also a small barn and plot of land to raise feed for the horses and the dairy animals, and to raise enough vegetables to keep the Guild self-sufficient.

Janna was neither a native nor a resident. Eldest daughter of the Hastur clan, she had served her time in a Tower, but declined Comyn marriage, and joined the Renunciates. She wanted to be her own woman, and her own woman she was. She had taken a cartwright in Thendara in freemate marriage, by whom she had children, and now, grandchildren. In her life, she had ridden as escort and bodyguard for many traveling Comyn ladies, been employed as a tracker, worked on the firelines, and, when necessary, spoke with members of the Comyn Council on issues relating to the Renunciates. When Mother Rayna, the Guild-mother here, had sent word to Thendara that a Renunciate had committed murder, and asked for aid, the Guild House in Thendara sent Janna.

"The widow had been beaten by her husband, hadn't she?" Janna said to Rayna as she hung up her cloak in the Guild House.

"Many a time," said Rayna, walking with Janna from the cloakroom to her own room. The Guild-mother was outfitted as Janna was, wearing trousers, a thick shirt, vest, and boots. "She was afraid to leave him, and I doubt she will mourn overmuch at his passing. But this is the second death in two tendays, and I fear that if we do not catch her soon, Comyn Council will make this their business, and our charter throughout the Seven Domains will be in danger." She sat in a chair by her fireplace, and motioned Janna to do the same.

Janna sat, only aware in that act that her muscles were tired and sore from the long ride, the brief stop at the Guild House, and the walk to and from the widow's house. She had not even taken off her traveling clothes, and had no idea where the other Guild-sisters had taken her baggage and horse.

"You said that after the first death, you ordered Liriel confined to the Guild House, and she escaped. That makes her an outlaw among us. You could lawfully hunt her down."

Rayna spread her arms. "Try to catch her." She ran a hand through her hair, as gray-streaked as Janna's own, except Rayna's basic color was black while Janna's was copper. "Liriel was willful and stubborn even as she came here. She is a nedestro of the Ridenow clan, raised in a village just north of here. She arrived at our step one day. Usually, kin come to inquire after the women who join us—either angrily, if the woman ran away, or to ask after their health, if the woman came with the family's knowledge. No one has ever come to ask after Liriel."

"If she was rebellious, why did you take her in?"

"She wasn't difficult—at least, not at first. She was determined to become a Renunciate, and served her homebound year with the single-mindedness she had for every task. There were no complaints about her. She was a good student at anything we taught her—especially swordplay. When she completed her year, she served the house well. But slowly, things began to happen. She would claim that one of her Guild-sisters had talked to her, and the woman would deny it. Then she said that she heard voices coming from the wells. The midwives told me that when they were in the woods, Liriel would claim that the trees and the sky spoke to her."

"What did you do?"

Rayna shrugged. "What could we do? We tried to keep her busy. That helped a little, but her constant talk about voices was wearing down the other sisters. I began to plan to send her to a Tower, to see if the leroni could help her, as they can sometimes with difficult illnesses. But before I could send a letter, Liriel went out one night and killed Alaric."

Janna shifted her weight in the chair. "Who was Alaric?"

"He was a ne'er-do-well who had a reputation in all the villages around here. Most parents would hide their daughters if they saw him. Some of the girls—and Alaric never chased women fully grown—said that he took them unwilling. But he would never stay around any place long enough for anyone to catch him. Liriel came in the door in the morning with blood on her clothes and announced that Zandru had appeared to her and told her to send Alaric to him. She was quite unruffled—changed her clothes, took a bath, and ate breakfast while the others sat at the table, too overwhelmed to speak."

Janna sighed.

"Not many missed Alaric," continued Rayna. "Some fathers of the girls Alaric had used said that Liriel had only done what they were thinking of doing. But I ordered her to stay indoors until I could write to the leroni. Before I got the letter drafted, Liriel escaped. That is when I sent one sister to the leroni and one to Thendara. You arrived first, and in the meantime, Liriel killed again."

Janna rubbed her forehead. "I served a term in a Tower. They have been sent cases such as this before. I think that you will hear back that they can do nothing. It may be better if she eats some wild poison herbs in the forest and the gods take her. She will endure a lifetime of suffering, otherwise—either chained so that she does not kill again, or out in the open, mindlessly taking lives until someone, at last, murders her."

There was a long silence. At last, Rayna said, "I am sorry. To be honest, Liriel was not a friend, but no matter how difficult the woman, I have never failed a Guild-sister in all my years. I feel that I have failed now."

"Worse," said Janna, "would be to do nothing. Many already have the image of Renunciates as perverts and bullies. Just one case of a murderer among us could ruin the Guild's reputation in the entire Seven Domains. Employers will no longer hire us, people will fear us even more, and there will be calls in Comyn Council to revoke our charter. This is something we must solve ourselves and quickly."

Rayna smiled. "Surely you can take time to rest after your journey, and eat a little?"

"Eat...a little, yes. Then I have to go out to find her before the trail is cold."

"I don't think she'll stray far," said Rayna.

"All the easier to catch her."

Janna started in the field of the widow's farm. Although the prints were a day old, they were not hard to spot, in the dried mud. The thick soles of the Renunciates' boots, made by sisters, were scored in a certain way to grip the earth better. The pattern was unmistakable. Janna looked up, reckoning that it was just past midday. If Liriel was still in the area, Janna ought to find her by nightfall. She stood, brushing the dust from her hands. Once she found the renegade, she would bring her back and put her in a locked room until Mother Rayna decided what to do with her. A nice day's work.

The prints led to the surrounding forest. Liriel was making no attempt to avoid being followed, judging by the trail she left behind. Janna reckoned it must have rained the day before she killed the second man, for the ground was dry now, but the prints were still discernible. They led to a place by a stream, well out of sight of the village, where there was a campfire and a crude lean-to fashioned out of tree branches and long grasses.

Liriel was pacing next to the campfire. She had not spotted Janna; the tracker crept forward, screening herself from her quarry by circling around from tree to tree. As she came closer, she heard Liriel talking to herself. Janna peered around a trunk, trying to make out the words.

Abruptly, Liriel stopped talking. Janna pulled her head back. She drew her sword, knowing Liriel was coming toward her by the sound of the boots swishing the grasses. When she judged Liriel was just behind the tree, she swung around, blade raised.

Liriel glared at her. Red curls hung over the other woman's large brown eyes. The face was smooth and unwrinkled, the hair without even a touch of gray. She was taller than Janna by half a head; her frame was sturdy, her expression stern.

"You could be named an outlaw for drawing steel on a sister," Liriel warned.

"It is you who are the outlaw, refusing to submit to the discipline of your Guild-mother."

Liriel straightened up proudly. "I obey the laws of the gods first, the Guild second. So I swore when I took my oath."

Janna altered her stance, although she kept a firm grip on the hilt of her unsheathed sword. Liriel did not rave. Perhaps, thought Janna, there was a corner of rationality that might be reached. "So you killed those two people on the orders of the gods?"

"Of course." Liriel's tone implied that she thought she was stating the obvious. "I admit I made a mistake in killing the first one, using my sword. Zandru did not tell me that there was another way. It was Avarra who told me how to kill bloodlessly, without a weapon—with my mind." She touched her forehead. "She has forgiven me for my error; as a Renunciate, I should not have listened to Zandru anyway. She has given me a new task. May Avarra herself judge me if I fail."

Janna was still trying to figure out exactly what Liriel had done with her laran. A telepath with the Alton Gift could kill with a thought—did she have the Alton Gift? Janna did not know. It took an Alton to test another Alton. She herself had the Hastur Gift. If Liriel was indeed a nedestro of the Ridenow clan, she ought to have the Ridenow Gift, manifested either in empathic contact or in communicating with alien intelligences. But that did not mean she could not have done what she claimed. Laran was a powerful weapon in itself.

Janna licked her lips, considering. "If, sister, your instructions indeed came from the gods, then Mother Rayna may see that she judged you in error. May I speak to them also? Then you will be free. Otherwise, your Guild-sisters will consider you an outlaw all of your life."

"You...?" Liriel obviously had not expected that request. Before the older woman could say anything further, Liriel turned her head abruptly, then back to face Janna. "Since you are a Hastur of Hasturs, they say you, too, may see them. Sheathe your sword and come." She walked toward the campfire.

Janna did as she was told, not because she trusted Liriel, but because the younger woman wore only a knife, and Janna had confidence that she could overwhelm Liriel if the two got into a fight.

Liriel stopped at the fire, pointing. "Look at the flame."

Janna saw nothing but fire. But she felt a tickle at her throat. Without prompting from Liriel, she uncovered her matrix, and focused her laran through that to look at the flame.

It was blinding. She dropped the matrix. The stone, at the end of its string around her throat, bounced against her sternum. She put her arm up to shield her eyes, but the light was in her mind, not her eyes. It would not rub out. It would not go away when she turned her head or closed her eyelids. It was everywhere, in her head, in her ears. The smell filled her nostrils. Her tongue tasted it. It invaded her very being, and then let her go, into darkness.

Janna opened her eyes. She was looking at stars. The light was framed by a circle of treetops. She was on her back. She turned. The campfire was nothing but dimly glowing embers. Liriel was gone.

Janna moaned and sat up. She felt her legs and arms. They appeared to be all right. Her head was not bruised or ringing. She seemed uninjured. She rubbed her forehead. There was a dull headache, as if a fever had abated, but that was not even a nuisance. She took a draught of the night air and let it out in a sigh. Catching Liriel was going to be more complicated than she thought.

She went back toward the village. Before she reached the first house, she heard a scream. Running to the sound, she saw a man, dead, on a doorstep. A woman stood over him, fingers stuffed into her mouth to muffle her own screams. Janna bent down to examine the body. It was Ruyvil. As with the victim she had seen earlier, there was not a mark on him.

Janna stood and saw Mother Rayna running up. "Did you see who did this, Gwynnis?" Rayna asked the woman on the doorstep.

Gwynnis pulled her hand from her mouth. "Na, na. I heard a thump on the step, and I thought it was Ruyvil, drunk again. I opened the door, and there he was."

A crowd was gathering. "I'll take care of my cousin," said a man who glared at the Renunciates.

Rayna and Janna exchanged a glance and walked back to the Guild House. "No doubt that this was Liriel's work," said Rayna when they were inside. She led Janna to the kitchen. She pulled out some apples and a cold meat pie and set them in front of Janna with a plate and fork. "Here, eat, you look like you just came from Zandru's seventh hell."

"Perhaps I have." Janna related the events of the afternoon while she ate. When she finished her meal, she added, "Either she has the Alton Gift, which she was projecting on me, or she has the Ridenow Gift, and she is in touch with something beyond this world, which she thinks are gods."

"Perhaps she is truly mad, and using ordinary laran to pass her delusions to you."

"Perhaps," mused Janna. "When I had my turn in the Towers, someone with unmanageable laran was brought to us. The Keeper there burned the laran centers from the brain, leaving the victim otherwise unharmed. The kindest thing to do would be to catch her and take her to a Tower."

"But can she be caught without further loss of life?" said Rayna. "She may fight you, and you may have to kill her. She is already an outlaw, according to our Guild rules."

Janna rubbed her eyes. "I don't know. I'd like to go out right now and find her...."

"No," said Rayna, thumping the table for emphasis.

Janna smiled. "...but I'm not as young as I used to be. I'll have to get a night's rest, and think it over. Perhaps morning will bring a solution."

"Good," said Rayna. "Since you are resolved on that, I have other news for you. While you were out this afternoon looking for Liriel, a message came to me from your brother in Thendara. The news of what has been happening here has reached the ears of Lord Serrais, and he is coming here with several Guardsmen. There are murmurings about revoking the Renunciates' charter in Council. Your brother is stalling, but he could not restrain Lord Serrais. If we don't trap Liriel soon, someone else will undoubtedly do it for us."

Janna nodded. "If he sent a message to you, he probably has also sent a message to Mother Margali at the Guild House in Thendara."

"It is nice to have a brother who supports the Renunciates."

Janna smiled. "Not all men are against us. I happened to marry one who wasn't."

By the time she pulled her boots on the next morning, Janna had a plan in mind. She ate breakfast with the other Guild-sisters in the house. Some offered to come with her. Janna thought that a search party would cause Liriel to run, or make it more likely that the renegade would kill or be killed. She declined their help with thanks.

The sisters in the kitchen packed a knapsack with food for her. She left her horse in the stable, and went on foot once more. At a distance from Liriel's camp—Liriel was at the same place she had been the day before—Janna sat under a tree. A bush shielded her from Liriel's eyes, but she could see Liriel through the small leaves. Janna turned, rested against the trunk, and ate some of the provisions she had brought. Once more, she peered through the brush. Liriel was still there, sitting by the campfire, mumbling to...herself.

Gingerly, as if the whisper of the silk might make a sound, Janna uncovered her matrix. When she worked in the Tower, she did a monitor's work. She knew how to regulate another's body rhythms from a distance. She had also been taught healing, and knew the innermost workings of the body. Most important, she knew where the laran centers of the brain were. If she could affect those somehow, perhaps she could free Liriel from the demons that possessed her. It was tricky, and Liriel might die as a result, but Janna was running out of alternatives. If she did not do something about Liriel, the villagers or Lord Serrais and his Guardsmen certainly would.

In the Domains, murder was considered largely a private affair, at least in the abstract, but Janna often found that popularly mouthed opinions were not observed in practice. The three men Liriel had killed would not be greatly missed, Janna suspected, by their victims. But because they died by a Renunciate's hand, rather than that of an outraged father or cousin, public indignation had spread even to Thendara. It confirmed what Janna had long concluded from experience: that killing a person, even a wicked person, often caused more problems than it solved. She was not about to complicate the matter by killing Liriel as well, not if it was in her power to do otherwise. Aside from that, Janna had never once harmed a Guild-sister, not even a renegade. She had a feeling inside her gut that to add Liriel to the dead, now, would be like cutting off an arm to get rid of a birthmark.

She assumed her monitor's posture, which should keep her muscles from getting cramped even if she sat there until sunset. Concentrating through her matrix, she found the network of energons that was Liriel's body. Carefully, so that Liriel would not be aware of it, Janna slowly probed the brain, reaching the laran center, isolating the cells....

No.

Janna eased back. Leaning to one side, she spotted Liriel, again, by the fire. The younger woman showed no sign that she was aware of the psychic probing. Janna must have imagined it; it must be her own nervousness. She shifted her weight, doing some breathing exercises to calm herself, and tried again.

There.

She had found the right cell group. Now, cell by cell, she could deaden that part of the brain.

Something grabbed her. No, it grabbed Liriel. No, it was the light again, the blinding light, in Liriel's psyche. Janna set her determination like a hook and pulled, feeling as if she were one of two banshees fighting over a piece of meat, only the meat was Liriel's laran. The adversary yanked. Janna saw, as if with her eyes, the forms, the figures, as Liriel saw them. They were bright beings, human in form.

Let her go! Janna said in Liriel's mind.

No, they replied. *We need this one to get our revenge.*

Revenge for what?

We died here, in a war. We have called and called for someone to answer us. This one has. We will use her to seek those who sent us here.

There has been no war here for generations. Those who killed you are long gone. The dead have no claim on the living.

Then we can kill their sons, and their son's sons.... Their anger burned like acid.

Janna flinched, but remained steadfast. The Altons were powerful, the Ridenows sensitive, but the Hasturs of legend had bound and banished even the gods. Janna uncloaked her Gift, matching their strength and brilliance. They pounded at her shields; Janna wavered, and then held steady. Something—someone was supporting her. Liriel. Her confidence bolstered, Janna rose over them, surrounded them, smothered them, and sent them back to the oblivion of the dead.

With a gasp, Janna was back in her body. Liriel was at her side, head on her shoulder. Weakly, Janna put an arm around her.

"I am sorry, my sister," said Liriel. "I will submit myself to whatever the Guild requires."

Janna used the last of her psychic strength to probe Liriel's brain. Part of the laran center was gone, but not all. "Do you still hear voices?"

"No. It's like I woke up from a nightmare."

Janna smiled. "I think you had the Ridenow Gift, but a far more sensitive one than any Ridenow has ever had. Your mind touched a presence no one should ever see." She kissed Liriel's head. "Don't worry; it's gone now."

"What do you think Mother Rayna will do?" she asked worriedly.

Janna hugged her. "Nothing as horrid as you might be imagining, I'm sure. I think that if you help me back to the Guild House, that will go a long way to erasing your debt." She moaned softly as Liriel helped her to her feet. With Liriel sane again, she had no doubt that the Guild could settle with the affected families, and that she, Janna, could convince Lord Serrais—and Comyn Council—that the Renunciates were in charge of their own. The honor of the Guild had been served.

An Invitation to Chaos

I felt as if I had just fought a battle. Comyn Council meetings were generally easy; Council Season was seen as more of a social occasion than a political one. No one expected any opposition to the proposal that the Keepers and workers in the Towers be allowed to sit and vote in council, but I was delighted to surprise them by objecting. It was an even bigger shock to them when the Domain of Alton split on the issue: me, the heir apparent to the Domain, in opposition, and my father, Lord Rafael Alton, just as strongly in favor. We argued to an impasse. The vote was delayed, which was a victory for me and a defeat for my father. I could almost hear the echoes in the now-empty Crystal Chamber. I sat back, put my feet up, and stared idly at the ceiling, savoring the moment.

"Admiring your handiwork?"

King Stefan Hastur reentered the chamber. Quickly, I put my feet down, but he motioned me to stay seated. With a smile, he walked to the Alton section and sat beside me.

I smiled back. Stefan and I were contemporaries. We were playmates as boys. I was fostered out for a year to Castle Hastur; he had been fostered out later to Armida.

"Quite a place you built," said Stefan. "If I had erected Thendara Castle, I think I might find a hill and gaze at it until I fainted from thirst."

I laughed. "That vain, I'm not. It just seemed to me that since all the Domain heads met here every year at the Thendara marketplace, we might as well make ourselves comfortable rather than camping out in the muck. Besides, it gave me something to do when I was penned up in that damned Tower."

"Ah," said Stefan, laying a finger to the side of his face. "So that's why you opposed the seating of the Tower Keepers in council—revenge."

"Revenge be damned," I said. "The telepath workers are getting too large for their clothes. I don't mind that they're organized so that they can do together what no telepath can do alone. But put them in Council and they'll begin to run Darkover, mark my words. They already want another Tower here at Thendara Castle, when I generously built them one as is. When my bones are moldering on the shores of Hali, that's when they'll add another Tower to this castle. I didn't build it for them; I built it so that they could serve us."

"You designed it, Gwynn. But they built it."

"They built it to my plan, and my specifications. I was in the Tower circle that erected it. They needed the power of my damned Alton Gift." I sat back. "That's all they're getting from me."

"Far be it from me to challenge the Alton Gift."

We both smiled. Stefan had the Hastur gift, awakened in him by his father before Stefan became king. As a child, Stefan had had white hair; it darkened into red as he grew older. He stood, tall and slender as a chieri, but, of course, he already had an infant son; he was no emmasca. I matched him in height, but I was the meatier one. Especially after leaving the Tower, I devoted myself to supervising the guards under Father's direction, and to other, more honest, physical work.

As we walked out of the chamber, Stefan said, "I wonder if you'd check out the mint for me. The city is growing so quickly, we'll need the coinage. Neskaya and Arilinn can't keep up."

"I'd be happy to, your highness." I executed a bow that was both properly respectful and a little playful. He turned a comer to the Hastur apartments.

I knew, of course, that Father was annoyed. Ever since he had imposed his damned Gift on my adolescent brain, I was aware of his every mood. Distance softened it to a low background murmur, but he was always there, as if he had scuffed my brain and left his scent on my mind forever.

He turned from his chair as soon as I walked in the door to the Alton apartments. His large, thick, red mustache would have looked ridiculous on any other man. On Father, it made him seem even larger and more powerful. The dark eyes in the huge face tried to pin me down, but I was almost oblivious to his physical appearance. It was the state of his laran that caught my attention.

He rose in a smooth motion. In a voice gentler than his mood, he said, "I don't blame you, son, not at all. I know what's really wrong."

"What?" I refrained from reading his mind which would have been easy under these circumstances.

"Dammit, son, do I have to spell it out? Get yourself a wife! It's about time!"

I turned away from him, stripping off my gloves and throwing them on a nearby table.

"All of your younger brothers and sisters have children already...."

"Good for them!" I tried to walk away; he followed me.

"What's wrong with you? You're not an ombredin; I would know if you were! You're 34 years old, and long past due! Now get yourself a woman before you make yourself sick! You don't have to marry one, though it would be nice if you would. Just get it over with! I don't think you've ever been with a woman, have you?"

I turned on him. "There are some things in my life that are out of your control, Father."

"I'm not going to stand by and let you ruin yourself. You're not an ordinary man; you're heir to Alton! Commander of the Guards! Builder of Thendara Castle! That disgraceful speech you gave today...."

"I meant every word!"

He thrust his finger in my face. "You wouldn't have proposed such an idiotic idea if you'd been married!"

"The reason why I've never bedded a woman is that I don't want you in there with me!"

"What do you mean, you...."

"You know what I mean! Ever since you gave me that damned Alton Gift, you've never been out of my mind!"

He put his finger in my face again. "I saved your life!"

I slapped his hand away. "You needn't have bothered. I was in no pain whatever. I was peacefully slipping into the arms of Avarra, when all of a sudden there was this excruciating pain in my head—you, Father!—tearing my mind into pieces. You left a little of yourself in there, and it's been there ever since, making my life a living hell. I would have been better off, dying of threshold sickness. I had younger brothers—you didn't need me for an heir. But no, you used the full force of your Alton Gift to bring me back, which, as an Alton heir, gave me the same damned thing, for which I had to leave home and live in that damned Tower with strangers, away from Mother and my brothers and sisters. Despite all the claptrap I hear about all the wonderful caring and sharing"—here I waxed sarcastic—"that comes from laran, all I felt was power. Raw power, and the stench of it made me want to vomit on my boots."

This was the first time in my life I had seen Father shocked speechless. He wasn't at a loss for long, however. "I loved you."

"You loved me? You ripped my mind apart, and then sent me away from home, from everything I loved...."

"An untrained telepath is a danger to himself and everyone around him."

"Oh, spare me! Stefan told me how his father had awakened his Hastur Gift, and taught him how to use it. Far different from my experience with you! Stefan's father loved him. What you did to me, you did for yourself!" I stomped past him, retrieved my gloves, and left, without going to my apartments and eating first, as I had planned. Father always had that effect on me, making me so angry I forgot everything except how much I wanted to get away from him.

"Gwynn?"

I stopped and turned. It was Michela, standing in the open doorway to the Aldaran apartments.

"Do you have a moment?" she asked.

In answer, I walked to the door. Michela was smaller than I was, in her early twenties. She was quite fetching; Stefan and I thought it probable that old Aldaran would arrange a marriage for her this council session.

"Would you come in?"

I smiled. "Certainly, damisela."

She led me to a parlor where a table was set for a meal. There were three plates, three chairs. Looking over to the hearth, I saw her father, Donal, Lord Aldaran, standing there.

He gestured to the table. "Will you join us, Lord Gwynn?"

"I was ready for a meal, thank you."

When we had been served, Aldaran said, "That was a good point you made in Council today. My daughter, here, who has the Aldaran Gift in full measure, has warned me that she has seen far into the future, and that if the Towers gain in power, there could be wars fought with terrible weapons."

"There is much more that can be done with laran than to simply communicate, or to build things, or to mine for metals," said Michela.

"I know," I said. "I have heard some say that they think they can breed for certain gifts, beyond the donas that lie within each Domain."

"If they try that," said Aldaran, "there will be many supporting you, and not just me. No one wishes to be bred like chervines." He took a sip of his drink. "I will back your position for as long as I am in council. Beyond the horrors that my daughter foresees, I will not let the Towers usurp my authority. I rule my Domain, and I will not be ruled by the laranzu'in."

"Are you planning to leave Council, sir?" I asked.

"No, not in the foreseeable future." Aldaran smiled at his unintentional joke, turning to his daughter. "But the journey is long from my home to Thendara. It has been useful and pleasant, gathering here every summer, to buy from the market and to exchange news and ideas with the other Domain lords. With your new addition, Gwynn," he looked around at the walls, "I find it even more comfortable, almost like a holiday. But the Towers have given us a faster way to run messages, and although I'm willing to acknowledge the Hastur king, I'm not going to put up with the Council very long if they're going to try to run my affairs." He gave me a knowing look. "Besides, my son is coming of age, and I intend to gradually hand the burden over to him. I look forward to an old age where my only care is how long I can bounce grandchildren on my knee." He smiled again at Michela.

By the gods, I wished the man was my father. He was firm without being tyrannical, kind without being patronizing. Most of all, there was nothing but a normal telepathic awareness of him, which I could overlook if I wished. My own father, on the other hand, was impossible to ignore.

We had a pleasant conversation over a pleasant meal. When we were finished, Aldaran retired. I lingered over my farewell to Michela—she was pleasant, like her father, had an unobtrusive telepathic presence, and was good looking, on top of that—and excused myself to run the king's errand.

Naturally, any excuse to go out in the city would do. Was there any man in the history of Darkover who could claim to have built such a city? The cobblestones of the street, the gutters below the walkways, the houses of both great and small, all carefully planned by me. Of course, it was not all matrix-built. Some of it was the result of good, honest labor. But the overall effect was just as beautiful as I had anticipated. In addition, I had left plenty of room for new buildings, taking thought for the future. In sum, Thendara was a thriving city, grown twice the size it was when I was a boy, and which would probably be twice the size it was now when I was old.

The most difficult task, of course, was the drainage system. There was no river of any size within easy walking distance. Standing puddles of rain, or worse, standing puddles of sewage, would invite plagues of insects and plagues of disease. At last, I created an underground conduit of stone and slate which brought everything to a large cave in the surrounding hills, where it would separate and filter into the silt and finally reach the streams that fed the River Valeron, and eventually go to the sea.

My destination that day, though, was the mint, newly created by King Stefan in deference to Thendara's growing importance as a trade and market center. With the almost unlimited potential of the Towers to mine metal, there was more wealth to go around—distributed carefully, of course. And that was another thing I had against the Towers: they could sit on that wealth like a dragon guarding its board. So far, they had obeyed the will of the king in these matters, but with them in Council, they could just as well try to reserve all such decisions for themselves.

For now, the mint was working well. All the mint workers were nonhuman kyrri, to whom the value of the metal meant nothing. Metal was so scarce, so frugally distributed, that it was too much of a temptation to anyone else. I saw that the metal was correctly mixed, with copper and silver in their proper proportions, that the ingots were all of standard size, and stamped according to size and composition; the sekals and reis coins were stamped correctly with King Stefan's visage. I tested the weights for the scales, which merchants bought from the mint in order to confirm that the ingots their customers used had not been shaved or adulterated. Everything was as it should be; the Thendara mint was the equal of the ones in Neskaya or Arilinn.

I went to a potter's shop next. I didn't really want to buy anything; I just visited every once in a while to see what they were using for slips and glazes, what sort of clay they were making pots out of, what designs they were using. I often got ideas for materials and shapes to use in my building projects. Little had changed since my last visit to this shop. However, a blue stone embedded in a pot caught my eye. I took it over to the proprietress, an older woman with a few missing front teeth.

"You really shouldn't be using matrix stones in your pots anymore, mestra. By the king's command, matrix stones must only be handled now by licensed matrix mechanics, Tower-trained. I know they're pretty, and you've used them for a long time, but they can be dangerous." The woman looked abashed. I felt awkward, too, but this new law was one I agreed with, whatever other differences I had with the Towers. I pulled out my purse. "Here. I'll buy this from you, and any other pots you might have with matrix stones in them. And then please don't use them anymore. Do you understand?"

"As you say, vai dom," she said, avoiding my gaze.

"Will you please check in your back storage for others? And please give me all the matrix stones you have, too." I touched my own matrix, which was in a pouch at my throat. "Don't worry about getting them all; I can check to see if you have missed or misplaced any."

Her face fell even more. "Yes, vai dom." She went into the back.

As usual for a Domain lord or a Domain heir going into the city on official business, I had a couple of retainers following at a discreet distance. I called them into the shop to take the pots back to the castle; I took the matrixes in hand. After checking to see I had all the matrixes in the shop, I paid the woman generously and left, thinking that I ought to ask King Stefan to have the Towers send some people into the city to collect more of the loose matrixes, especially among potters and jewelers.

It would give the Tower workers something useful to do for a change.

We left the shop, but outside the door one of my men slipped, and almost dropped the pots. As I helped him rearrange the burden, I heard the old woman's low complaint, probably to the younger woman who had been helping her. Doubtless the woman thought I had walked well out of earshot by now, but I caught every word.

"Those Comyn, they take the best of everything! It isn't enough that they sit in their nice houses with their metal forks and spoons while us plain folk have to make them out of wood and clay! Now they want our pretty blue stones, which are hard enough to come by as is, without them taking those, too! And those were my quickest-selling pots, my prettiest!" The woman wept softly.

As we walked away, I felt sorry for the old woman, but took comfort in the fact that I had paid her far more than the pots were worth. Besides, there were jewels other than matrix stones she could use, and other ways to make pots attractive. If she was as clever a potter as her pots showed that she was, she would not be going out of business over the loss of the matrix stones.

I reported the condition of the mint and the incident at the pottery shop to Stefan. Unexpectedly, the king showed more interest in the matrixes at the pottery shop. Seated in his overstuffed chair, he waved a hand at me from across the rug. "Of course, now that we have Towers to deal with them, the matrixes have to be kept out of the hands who do not know how to use them. But it wasn't all that long ago that there were no Towers, and to nontelepaths, matrixes were just jewelry." He shifted from leisurely sag to a straighter, more kingly posture. "My great-grandsire, for instance, had a special sword made for him by the forge-folk in the Hellers. In the hilt is a rather large matrix. He had it made for ceremonial occasions, but the matrix made it feel so...alive...that he kept it in a vault in Castle Hastur nearly all the time. It hasn't seen the light of day in years, except in the passing on of the Hastur Gift."

"Have the Towers seen it?" I asked, interested. "I mean, when you were tested for the Hastur Gift."

He had a conspiratorial look on his face. "No. They tested me later, at Hali. When my father awakened the Hastur Gift in me, it was a ceremony only between the two of us."

"Don't tell them," I urged. "They'll take it from you for certain."

"I have no intention of telling them. The only reason I'm telling you is that you are the one person it is safe for me to tell." He smiled.

The rest of the summer went better than I expected. The debate on whether to allow the Tower workers a voice in Council went on without a consensus being reached, though more and more were being won to my way of thinking every day. Most of the Council session dealt with the usual: mountain bandits, road repair and transportation, harvest expectations, and so forth.

Outside the Council, I spent most of my time in the Aldaran apartments. I had become more and more attached to Aldaran and Michela, and they seemed equally fond of me. My engagement to Michela became official at midsummer. Lady Aldaran and Michela's younger brother came for the occasion, as did my mother, from Armida. Mother seldom came to the Council sessions because of the inevitability of Father and me arguing when at close quarters. Mother always felt caught in the middle, and found it easier to avoid us both. In fact, when at home, Father and I were seldom in the same room at the same time; things were more civil that way.

Watching Father talk to Aldaran as if the two were pledged bredin almost made me sick. I shut down my laran, for courtesy's sake. Michela could tell something was wrong, but didn't ask right then. She left with her father at the end of the reception. Mother could also see storm clouds above my head; she excused herself, leaving Father and me alone.

Before I could say anything, Father swung around to face me. "Dammit, son, can't you contain your anger for your own betrothal party? It's supposed to be a happy occasion. I can't understand what you're upset about."

"That's the problem—you don't understand," I snapped. "And I controlled my laran just fine. The only reason you picked up on it is because we're linked, mind to mind."

"Then why can't I tell what's bothering you?"

"Because I'm blocking my laran, that's why. But if you weren't so deliberately blind to my feelings, you could tell what's wrong. What's wrong is that you treat total strangers with more courtesy than you do me, your own son." I thumped my chest for emphasis. "You don't speak with Aldaran except once a year, and you treat him as if he was your long lost beloved brother. Me, on the other hand, you treat like property!"

"And how about the way you treat me...the way you're speaking to me right now?"

"If you'd shown me half the courtesy you showed Aldaran, we wouldn't be having this discussion. But no, you act as if the world is centered around you. You imposed your Alton Gift on me because that is what you wanted. You sent me to a Tower because that is what you wanted. I only got out of the Tower because you thought it was time to learn how to command the Guards. You tell me that I'm to run the Domain someday, but you do all the running of it. King Stefan gives me more responsibility than you do. If you were to drop dead tomorrow, I would only know how to run the Domain because Stefan has taught me how to do it. The only thing you do is give orders and expect me to carry them out. You pull me around like a cralmac on a chain, and then you wonder why I'm angry when you show Aldaran more courtesy than you do me?"

He looked genuinely puzzled. I could tell, with my laran, that he was genuinely confused, which irked me even more. "I let you choose your future wife, didn't I? Some Domain lords would introduce you to your bride on your wedding day."

I executed a mock bow. "Thank you, thank you very much," I said sarcastically. "And let me tell you, one of the reasons I'm marrying her is that Aldaran has been more of a father to me than you have, even in the short time I've known him. Since you think he's such a wonderful man, why don't you ask him how to do it?" Without waiting for an answer, I turned my back on him and went to my own room.

He did not pursue the matter.

I really did not know what I was going to do when my wedding night came. Ever since I acquired the Alton Gift, I was always aware, on some level, of my parents' lovemaking. I learned to block it out, but the fact that such knowledge was available to me, unbidden, bothered me. I presumed that the reverse would be true as well: that if I ever made love, my father would know about it. That's why I was still a virgin at my age.

To prepare, I tried to get physically intimate with Michela at levels just short of lovemaking. We would sit for hours, side by side on a couch in a parlor in the Aldaran apartments, with Michela's deaf maid, Ariel, doing embroidery across the room under the light of a lamp. Ariel was a nedestro daughter of the Ardais domain, and had laran, which greatly helped her to communicate with her Aldaran employers, though she could use gestures to speak, as well.

One night, as Michela and I were enjoying each other's company, my head on her shoulder, I suddenly gasped and straightened. Ariel had lowered her embroidery, and cocked her head as if actually listening to something.

"What was that?" asked Michela.

I stood. "I don't know, but I'm going to find out."

Before I could take a step, there was a knock at the door. Aldaran stuck in his head. "It's the Tower, son; let's go. Michela, you stay here."

We stepped into the corridor and found ourselves in a procession with King Stefan at the head, flanked by his bodyguards. Every person with laran in Thendara must have sensed the same thing. I knew something they didn't: that my father was also a part of whatever we had felt.

I was in the front with Stefan by the time we got to the Tower. The king went right into the Tower's public rooms. My father and the Keeper of the first circle, a man named Edric, met us.

"There is no cause for worry, your majesty," said Edric. "Our experiment just got out of hand, that's all. We'll shield it better the next time."

"What sort of experiment?" asked Stefan.

"Weather control," said Edric. "It would serve us well in fire season if we could move rain clouds to the affected areas."

"We had just not anticipated the amount of shielding needed, your majesty," said my father, "and there was a certain amount of leakage. It won't happen again."

"Were you successful?" asked Stefan.

"A little," said Edric. "It was our first try. Perhaps we used more power than we needed. We weren't able to direct it as we had hoped; that caused the discomfort you felt. Again, I apologize."

The king's expression was stern. His voice, when he spoke, was softer. "I think it would be best if you halted your experiments for the next tenday. You also might take more time to plan your projects before you begin them."

"But we do, majesty," protested Edric. "And we can't stop our experiments. Mining, at first, was an experiment. So was matrix healing. So was building at an architect's direction." He gestured toward me.

"Leave me out of this," I said.

"I'm not asking that you stop trying things out," said Stefan. "I'm commanding that you cease your experiments for a tenday. I also insist that you plan your operations more carefully. You should try out things gradually: do things on a small scale before proceeding to more powerful uses of laran."

"But we do this already," said Edric.

"If so, what went wrong tonight?" asked Stefan.

Edric was silent. He looked to my father, but he said nothing, either.

"If you can't control your experiments or be consistent in what you do, be assured that the crown will step in," said Stefan. "My order stands: no more experiments from this Tower for the next tenday."

"Yes, majesty," said Edric.

Stefan turned to the assemblage of Domain heads and Domain heirs who had accompanied us to the Tower. "I will be retiring to Castle Hastur for a short time; Lord Gwynn will preside over the Council in my absence." Stefan touched my shoulder. "That will be all for now."

The others turned to go. Stefan held my elbow to keep me with him.

"Tell Michela I'll be along shortly, Father," I said to Aldaran. Aldaran nodded and left. I sensed, rather than saw, my own father gape when I called Aldaran that. His mouth was closed by the time I had turned around, with Stefan.

"Good evening, then," said the king, nodding at my father and Edric.

Stefan and I walked back to the Hastur apartments alone. "Yes, the Towers do need a tight rein on them. I think the debate will turn to your favor now, Gwynn."

"I noted that they deemed it necessary to have my father helping them," I said.

"...the Alton Gift, yes, the most powerful laran among us," said Stefan. "That was my thought, too."

"May I ask why you're returning to Castle Hastur?"

He rubbed his fingertips with a thumb. "Something I need...." he said, but he elaborated no further.

Stefan came back with a wooden case the size of a coffin. He put it in a storage room under a personal matrix lock and stationed two guards in front of it at all times. He lifted his ban on the matrix experiments. Meanwhile, the Council debate got hotter. Although no Keepers were allowed a voice in council, there were Domain lords and Domain heirs and others allowed to speak in council who were former or current Tower workers. My father was their chief spokesman. They maintained that the Towers already had a code of conduct, which was being changed and improved as their knowledge and experience grew. Matrix work was a science, they claimed, and could not be fully understood by people not familiar with that science, and should not be regulated by those who did not understand those principles. Ultimately, they said, Keepers should not be responsible to anyone or anything but their own consciences.

The opposition, which I led with vigor, countered that as long as what the Towers did affected the people and lands of Darkover, then the Domain heads, and the king, who were responsible for the people and lands of Darkover, had the right to lay down the rules for what the Towers could and could not do. To allow the Towers to do anything they wished, we believed, would be an invitation to chaos. Self-regulation with the Towers was the same as no regulation, we argued, because then the Towers would simply do as the pleased, answering to no one, and bearing no responsibility to anyone outside the Towers for their actions.

While this discussion went on, day after day, my father and I grew more estranged, which I had not thought possible until it happened. My mother, fed up with the situation, returned to Armida. Aldaran arranged to quietly move my things from the Alton apartments and into the guest quarters of the Aldaran apartments. While my father and I still sat in the same section in the Crystal Chamber, it was as if we were in different domains. I addressed him as "Lord Alton," and he addressed me as "Lord Gwynn."

Stefan and I had anticipated that the Towers, especially Thendara Tower, would try some outlandish experiments, in the fear that their activities would soon be tightly restricted by the Council. Whatever they were doing, however, they appeared to be doing it carefully. There was no more leakage. I was suspicious of the quiet, but Stefan reasoned that if they were careful enough to prevent leakage, they were probably using caution in other areas as well, and left them alone for the moment.

Late summer was the height of the fire season. Thendara itself was in little danger. The city walls would keep fire from the town, and the surface mining that had been done in the Venza hills before the Towers started mining had left areas of barren ground, acting as natural firebreaks. Therefore, whenever a fire was sparked in the country surrounding Thendara, no alarm was sounded.

That was why, when smoke was spotted on one of the hills, I took Michela to an observation post on the roof of the castle to watch it burn. Stefan joined us.

"No clouds in the sky," I said. "It must have been a careless hunter, whose fire had not been covered properly. It could have smoldered for days before igniting the brush."

Suddenly, a gust of wind lifted us up and threw us against a parapet. Stefan and I each grabbed one of Michela's arms and struggled to the doorway. Inside, out of reach of the gale, Stefan said, "What in Zandru's seven hells was that?"

My unending link with my father told me. "The Tower circle is in operation. I think they're trying to blow it out."

"They're...."

Stefan did not complete his sentence. A hideous sound stilled his voice. I had heard the banshees cry in the Hellers; that was a lullabye compared to this. Michela stopped her ears with her hands. Stefan bounded down the stairs.

Using my matrix, I got a clearer contact with my father. Indeed, they had been trying to blow out the fire, but it had gotten out of control. My father had not just put the Alton Gift into the wind, but also his resentment and anguish at my rejection of him into the circle. There was not just wind out there—it was a wind demon, composed of Alton anger, driven by Alton power. Realizing what he had done, my father was now trying desperately to reverse it, with the help of the others in the circle.

I knew it was dangerous to break into a circle, but my father and I were already deeply in rapport, and my telepathic eavesdropping had not affected the circle thus far. I lent my strength to theirs. But my father thrust me away, with such force that I was dimly aware of my feet buckling under me. My shoulder hit the inside wall of the parapet and I slid to the floor.

I was not going to let him push me away so easily. With a renewed grip on my matrix, I tried to reestablish contact, but was blocked. Trying another approach, I thrust into the overworld, the psychic plain mirroring physical events in the real world. There I saw that my father had thrust not just me, but all in the circle away, while he battled alone with the demon's surrogate in the overworld. We all tried to get to him, but it was as if there was an impregnable wall between us. Father matched the demon, strength for strength, height for height. They grappled.

I was no longer looking at the embodiment of my cursed gift tackling a monster of his own creation. Instead, I saw Darkover, personified, fighting against a Tower-made weapon for domination of the world. If the demon won, all of Darkover would be in chaos.

Linked together with the other Tower workers, I broke the barrier that Father created to protect us. Immediately, the demon grew, drawing from our combined strength. Realizing that we were only making the demon stronger, Edric dissolved the Tower circle. I remained, reaching out to snatch Father from the demon's grip, but the beast—now doubled in size—hurled Father to the floor of the psychic plain, smashing the astral form.

The shock of my father's death threw me out of the overworld. Back in my own body, I gradually became aware that I was staring at a stone ceiling. I could hear the howl of triumph of the wind demon outside.

Stefan bent down and touched my shoulder. "Come, Gwynn, before it gets to the castle gate."

My castle. My city. They were in danger. I stood. For the first time, I noticed that Michela was still there.

Stefan unwrapped a package. The matrix at his throat glowed so brightly I could see it clearly through its spider-silk wrappings. "Have you ever worked with other telepaths?" he asked Michela.

She nodded and touched the matrix at her own throat.

"Good." Stefan lifted the sword in his hand, as if testing its balance before a fight. He nodded at me, then Michela. "Let's go."

I opened my mouth to tell him that standing outside in the demon wind was impossible, but he was already out the door, Michela at his elbow. I sprinted out behind him. He waved the sword as he stepped out. Around us, the wind crashed against the parapet like a mighty wave, but the air where we were was calm. Stefan glowed. A nimbus surrounded him. He laughed as a man laughs when he goes into a fight, confident of victory. Before my eyes he was transformed: he took the shape of the legendary Hastur, son of light, so real that the images I had seen in Castle Hastur looked like childish scrawls in comparison. I almost knelt. Without touching me, the champion took me in hand, and, together with Michela, we faced the demon as it strode toward Thendara Castle and the city gates. Stefan matched the demon, strength for strength, height for height, power for power. The wind-demon roared angrily. Stefan stepped forward and extended the sword.

In words that rose over the demon howl and echoed among the castle rocks, Stefan ordered, "Begone! Go back to the hell that spawned you!"

Immediately there was calm. If it had not been for the leaves and debris scattered around, ripped from the trees and bushes, I would not have believed that there had been any wind. Then I saw that we were not on the roof of Thendara Castle, but on the plain in front of the city gates. I turned to Michela. She looked fine, though bewildered. I swung around in the other direction to find Stefan. He was there, in his normal shape, with a smile on his face. It took me a few moments to tell what had changed—Stefan's hair had turned back to the white color it had been when he was a young boy.

"I think the Council will approve your proposal now, don't you think?" said the King.

Mother returned for Father's funeral, as did my scattered brothers and sisters. We buried him in an unmarked grave by the shores of Lake Hali, beside the newly-erected vault of my design in which we placed Stefan's sword—behind double-barriers to keep it from the hands of the Towers. I finally cried at Father's funeral, but not for the man who invaded my mind and lived there afterwards. I wept for the man who read to me as a boy, soothed my fears, tucked me into bed, and for the man, who, at the last, saw the horror that he had created and had tried to stop it. But most of all, Father's death left me with a great sense of relief, as if I had been bound in irons all my adult life, and had been newly freed.

I was installed as Lord Alton in Council, and won my fight to bar the Tower Keepers from a voice or vote there. My triumph was further sweetened by my marriage to Michela. Stefan locked the catenas on our wrists himself. This, however, felt not like a binding, but as a seal of our affection.

That night, when all the others had gone, I made love with my whole heart. Afterward, we lay in each other's arms, and talked.

"I hope that I don't offend you by saying this, husband," Michela said, "but I do believe that in spite of everything, your father loved you."

I sighed. "Yes. He did love me. I can see that now, but not when my mind was chained to his. We were so—damnably—close, I think it was impossible for us not to strike sparks when we were together. And Father's attitude didn't help—he thought that as long as he knew he loved me, he didn't have to do anything to show it." I took a breath. "If we are ever in danger of losing children to threshold sickness, I will do anything—but I will not force the Alton Gift on them. No child of mine will suffer that kind of hell."

Michela caressed my forehead. "Gwynn...that wind-demon we fought...that is not what I saw in my foresight. I saw more hideous weapons than these, created by the Towers for war."

I caught her hand and kissed her fingertips. "Be at peace, my love. None of that will happen while Stefan and I live. All we can do is to be sure that none of us call up such horrors, and teach our children not to create them. What our children or children's children do when our bones are dust is not ours to command."

"I know. But the images are no less disturbing."

For that, I had no answer.

The Mystery Woman of the Kilghard Hills

Young Kennard Lanart sat on the grassy hillside to catch his breath. His brother, Lewis-Valentine, and his foster sister, Dorilys, had run too far ahead for him to catch up. He could no longer see them through the woods and the thick underbrush. But above the trees, he could see the tops of the walls surrounding his Armida home. They were probably in the house by now, snatching pieces of fresh-baked sweets from the kitchen folk.

A pair of antlers stuck up among the grasses, rocking back and forth as they moved across Kennard's path. Cautiously, Kennard crept forward. Two paces away from the antlers, he stopped. A rabbithorn mother was leading her brood through the woods. The young ones only had bumps where horns would later grow. Kennard counted five babies.

A tiny rustling made him turn. Another rabbithorn was tangled in thorns, unable to extract itself. Kennard took his gloves from his belt—his father had give him the gloves last winter on his seventh birthday—and walked over to the thornbush.

"So your brothers and sisters left you behind, too?" Kennard said softly. Gently, without touching the entangled creature, he parted the thorns with his hands. The rabbithorn, only slightly scratched, quickly hopped after its siblings.

Something larger rustled the branches uphill from Kennard. A chervine? They were about as big as a horse, and had antlers like a rabbithorn, only larger. Kennard shifted his weight back and forth, straining to see, but there was too much brush and too many trees between him and what was making the noise. Or maybe Lewis and Dorilys had doubled back, to sneak up from behind and scare him?

The noise continued, but no one appeared. Kennard put his hands on his hips. "All right! I know you're there. Just come out. I'm not walking up there." The rustling stopped. Kennard took a step toward where he last heard the noise. "I said I'm not coming up there."

A large red shape leapt out at him. Kennard got the swift impression of a melon head covered with scraggly hair before he turned and ran, screaming, to the gates of Armida.

One of the guards at the gate, Edric, caught Kennard about the waist, swung him off his feet, and set him back down. "Here, now, what is it, young Ken? Bandits?"

"I don't know," said Kennard. "This thing came at me." He had had such a brief glimpse that even the impression he had was fading, and he found he could not describe it.

Edric motioned to two other men. "We'll have a look," he told Kennard. "Let me take you in to your father and tell him, in case there are bandits outside."

The family had settled in the Great Hall by the time Edric returned. Kennard's father Valdir sat in a soft chair, reading a book; Elorie, Kennard's mother, embroidered a shirt nearby. Lewis and Dorilys worked on puzzle pieces spread on the floor. Kennard did not feel like putting a puzzle together, and he found reading hard since he had to hold books at arm's length just to make out the letters. Instead, he arranged his toy guardsmen on the table in various fighting positions.

"We've searched the woods all around Armida, Lord Alton," said Edric to Valdir, "but we've seen nothing. It's possible that your son saw a chervine or a cralmac out of its territory. There are no signs of bandits, and no word of any in the nearby villages. We'll keep a close watch for the next day or two just in case, though."

Valdir nodded. "Thank you."

"Maybe Kennard saw that mysterious woman that Mirella told us about," volunteered Dorilys.

Elorie looked up from her needlework and smiled. "Don't tell me you believe Mirella's tale about that woman with the spindly fingers who snatches disobedient children and eats them for supper," she said. "She was scaring your Uncle Valdir with those stories when he was a child."

Valdir turned to Lewis and Dorilys. "Now you see why I told you children not to separate, even in sight of these walls?

What if there had been bandits in the hills? We might never have seen Kennard again."

Lewis looked down at the floor as he answered, "We didn't mean to lose him. He just didn't keep up."

Elorie and Valdir exchanged knowing glances. Valdir said, "It will be a while before I let you out of these walls without an escort. And Kennard can go ask the kitchen folk for an extra plate of sweets, while you two go without. Maybe you'll think again before leaving your brother to fend for himself."

The kitchen folk let Kennard sit on the counter with a jar of baked sweets at his side. He listened to their talk as he ate.

Janna, the head cook, patted Kennard's leg with a thick hand. "Don't feel too hard about Lewis leaving you out in the woods. He loves you none the less, he's just showing off for your cousin Dorilys. After she's been here a while, he'll go rock-hunting or butterfly-chasing with you as he always did."

Kennard shrugged. He was annoyed at Lewis for leaving him behind, but it had not been the first time, Dorilys or no, and besides, Kennard felt much better now that he could eat his fill.

"What do you think he saw?" asked Liriel, as she washed up the pots and plates from the midday meal.

"Oh, not Mirella's mysterious woman, to be sure," said Janna, taking her cleaning cloth to a flour-dusty counter. "That tale was old in my granddam's time."

"When I was at my mother's a tenday ago," said Fiona, who rinsed and dried the dishes and gave them to Tani to put away, "she told me a woman came to her village not long ago, begging for rags, and asking to trade dolls for thread and a bit of food. She was a bit confused, my mother said, but the dolls were beautifully sewn. Some of the little girls in the village pestered their mothers for the dolls, and the woman got what she wanted and went away."

"Why," said Tani, reaching to put the clean plates on a high shelf, "that sounds a bit like the story my sister told me of a woman come to her town, only she told fortunes for food."

"Ah, that's it, then," said Janna, putting a hand on her back and straightening up, "young Kennard here saw nought but a peddler woman."

"It didn't look like a peddler woman," Kennard mumbled.

Janna patted Kennard's shoulder. "Well, you were startled, chiyu. A brief glance in an unguarded moment could make a stout tree look like a giant with a battle ax."

Several leroni had stopped at Armida on their way from visiting kin in the Ridenow lands to their home at Arilinn Tower. After joining in the formal greetings, the three children left Valdir and Elorie talking to the guests. Kennard was aware that the adults hoped that each child would grow up with laran, but to Kennard, this business about reading minds was mostly boring grownup stuff. He was glad when the adults let them go.

Lewis and Dorilys quickly ran out of sight, down a long corridor and around a corner. Kennard did not even try to follow. He walked to the barn to see his pony. As he stroked the animal's sides, Bard, the horsemaster, walked up.

"Deserted again, young Kennard?"

The boy shrugged.

"Well, if it makes you feel any better, lots of boys Lewis' age show off when there are girls around. When you're a year or two older, you may find yourself doing the same thing."

Kennard went on stroking the horse.

"Why not saddle up and get some exercise? Whatever startled you hasn't come back, and since the worst of winter's so close now, there shouldn't be any bandits around. I'm sure the guardsmen at the gate will let you go just up the road and back."

As Kennard trotted out, Edric simply called to him not to ride too far and to come back soon. The day was sunny and the horse seemed glad for the air. Beyond the first bend of the road a woman wearing a dirty red-plaid skirt sat on the grassy bank, sewing. Kennard reined in the horse and turned. He saw Edric at the gate, but the guard could not see the woman because the hill's foot, which had caused the road to take a turn, blocked his view. Kennard decided it was safe enough to approach her. He was within shouting distance of Edric, and besides, he had his horse and his knife, plus his short sword that his father was teaching him to use. He dismounted and led the horse to where the woman sat.

The woman did not look up. Her oily hair, which could have been light brown or light red, fell forward over her face. Kennard wondered how she could see. He leaned back a little to get a clearer view. Her fine stitches outlined a beautiful eye on the rag head, a head stuffed with fresh-smelling grass.

The woman rocked back and forth as she stitched. "Want me to tell your fortune?" she asked. The voice was soft and clear, not old and cracked, as Kennard half-expected.

Kennard glanced back the way he came to reassure himself that he could get away quickly if he wished. "I...I don't have any money with me."

"Din't ask for none." She took the needle and rag doll in one hand. "Saw you before, but you ran off 'fore I could tell you nothing." Still rocking, she patted the ground beside her with the other hand.

Kennard sat about a pace away from her, holding tightly to the reins. There was enough slack for the horse to graze.

The woman edged closer. "Tell your future?"

He shrugged.

She reached inside her blouse. He could not see what she took out, but a blue glow came from her cupped hands. She concentrated for what Kennard thought was a long time. "See a wife and two boys for you," she said at last.

"But that's my mother and father and Lewis and I."

She shook her head. Her hair, long and in disarray, still covered her face. She reached back in her blouse.

Kennard heard horses' hooves on the road and turned. The leroni and their escort were leaving Armida. He pulled his horse to the side of the road and watched as they passed by. When they had gone, he looked back at the hill behind him. The woman had disappeared. He opened his mouth to call, but realized he did not know her name. Looking down, he saw the doll with the half-finished face. The one eye stared up at him. The woman might come back for it, but he hated to leave it on the ground. Resolving to give it back to the woman later, he picked it up and stuffed it deep inside his jacket.

"Father, what's it like to have laran?"

Valdir put down his book. "You can tell what people are thinking, or feeling, for one."

The boy shifted his weight uncomfortably. He knew only too well that his father often sensed what he thought or felt.

Valdir smiled. "I suppose you meant something more, such as what the leroni do?"

Kennard nodded.

Valdir reached into his shirt. The gesture was nearly the same one the woman on the road had used. Kennard watched, stunned. But his father did not seem to notice. He brought out a silk bag at the end of the necklace he always wore.

"I'm going to show you something. Don't touch it, though." Cautiously, Valdir opened the bag and allowed a small blue stone to spill into his cupped hand. Pointedly keeping his hands behind his back, Kennard craned his neck to see the stone better. It glowed.

"This is a matrix," said Valdir. "It is keyed to me, and it responds to my thoughts. But it is not very powerful. It can only do little things, such as making something look as if it is something else for a moment. The leroni have much larger ones in the towers where they work. By concentrating their laran on a big matrix, they can do wonderful things, like move clouds or rocks."

As Valdir rewrapped the matrix and put it back, Kennard asked, "Where do you get one of these?"

"Matrix mechanics, specially trained, keep matrixes. The leroni have more. When your laran awakens, we will find a leronis or a matrix mechanic, and see that you get one."

"How can I tell when that happens?"

Valdir smiled. "You can tell. When it seems to you that you can tell what people are thinking before they say it, you will know."

"When will that be?"

"Oh, maybe when you're ten or twelve. But don't worry about it...it will come."

"So I would have to go to a leronis to get a blue stone?"

"Yes." Valdir paused. "Matrixes used to be found in the ground, but those places have long since been mined out. I suppose it's possible to find a loose one now and again, if a matrix mechanic spills a box of them, for instance. There could also be some lying around ancient burial sites, or near ruins from the Ages of Chaos. But I wouldn't go hunting for them. You could look long and hard for a lifetime before finding one."

"Can people with laran tell fortunes?"

"Some can see the future, yes. There's a little of that gift in our family. I saw you and Lewis before you were born. "

Kennard flinched. Maybe the woman had seen his future, after all.

Valdir grinned. "It's nothing to be afraid of. Many people have it. You'll get so used to it, you won't remember when you didn't have it."

The next day, Kennard saddled his pony to go riding again. The sky was only cloudy when he had walked into the barn, but when he rode out, a hard wind pelted his face with snow.

"No going riding today, young Kennard," said Edric. "There's a blizzard coming."

"I'm not going far."

Edric shook his head. "No, I've seen snows come so thick you could get lost between the house and the barn. Better take your pony back and ride some other time."

"But what if someone's out there?"

"There are travel shelters all around, and several villages nearby. Anyone out in the open will find a thick stand of trees and huddle under the branches. I've done it once or twice myself."

When Kennard came out of the barn again, he could barely see the house through the snow. Edric took him by the arm. "Let me walk you to the door."

A human-sounding howl cut through the storm. Kennard froze.

"It's just the wind," said Edric.

The wind outside rattled the windows in the Great Hall, but Kennard paid no attention as he sat looking out, face close to the panes.

Lewis and Dorilys played a child's version of castles next to the hearthfire. "Come on, Ken," Lewis called. "You'd think you had never seen a blizzard before. "

Kennard shook his head.

After a time, Kennard sensed his father walk up behind him. Valdir sat on a sill, facing the boy. "What's troubling you, son? Did you leave something out there?"

Kennard did not know what his father would say if he told him about the woman. On the other hand, it was nearly impossible for him to keep things from his father. He brought out the doll from his indoor jacket and gave it to Valdir.

Elorie saw the motion, put down her embroidery, and walked over. "That's beautiful. Did one of the servants' daughters sew it for you?"

"But it's not done yet," said Dorilys, who had hurried over with Lewis.

"What are you doing with a doll anyway?" said Lewis.

"It's not mine, she dropped it!" said Kennard. "I took it to give it back to her."

Valdir touched Kennard's shoulder. "Who gave it to you?"

Kennard shrugged. "There was an old woman. I think the same one that chased me the other time. She had a blue stone like yours and she told me my future."

"Why didn't you tell us about this?" asked Elorie, concerned.

"I don't know. The kitchen folk said they heard about a peddler woman with dolls. I thought it was her."

"I haven't heard of a peddler with a matrix," said Valdir, looking over Kennard's shoulder to Elorie.

Elorie shook her head.

"Let me keep the doll for now," said Valdir. "I'll get in touch with Dorilys' father and see if there's something we can do."

When the blizzard had ended, Kennard rode out of Armida with his father, Edric, and a few other guardsmen. Dorilys's father, Kennard's Uncle Damon, met them on the road, with his and Lewis's Aunt Ellemir. Valdir had used his matrix to talk with them during the blizzard—Kennard was not quite sure how that worked.

Damon led them to a spot on the road and signaled for a halt. Kennard dismounted along with the others. Valdir and Damon crouched down beside him at the side of the road.

Damon put a gloved hand on Kennard's shoulder. "Do you understand what you need to do?"

Kennard nodded and took out the doll. "I try to get her to come here with me."

Ellemir bent over him. "I'd think she'd like it if you called her by her name—Margali. She's been lost for a very long time and this is the first chance we've had to find her."

Kennard felt himself blush. Valdir had told him all that, of course, about how Margali had been fathered by a man with laran who had died before marrying her mother. Margali's mother had married another man, and because neither had laran, there was no one to teach her about laran when it had awakened in her. Her father had been a matrix mechanic and had left a matrix with her mother to give to any offspring of their union. But with no one to teach or guide Margali, her mind had grown confused. Turned out by her parents, she wandered from place to place, avoiding the monitors sent from the leroni who had seen an unaccounted-for matrix in use from their Tower screens. All of it was so very complicated that Kennard had not understood everything, and had even forgotten the name.

"I'm sure you'll do just fine," said Damon. He pointed into the forest. "She's over there, just beyond the hill."

Kennard took the half-finished doll and waded through the powdery snow. Looking down from the hilltop, he saw nothing. Could his Uncle Damon be wrong? A pile of branches rustled. He caught a glimpse of a red plaid skirt. Slowly, he walked toward the rude shelter.

The branches parted. Margali ducked out, hair in front of her face as before. Kennard held out the doll out stiffly, as if it were a shield. The doll shivered in his hand.

Margali did not notice. "Oh, you brought my baby back." She took the doll and cuddled it.

"Would...would you like to see my pony? She's very nice."

"Not now. Saw before." She sat. Bringing out a needle and thread from a pocket, she began to finish the face.

"My mother said that was very good sewing."

"I sew good babies. Treat my babies nice, as a mother should, and give my babies to mothers who love them, as babies should be given."

Kennard shifted his weight. "Yes," was all he could think of to say.

She looked him straight in the eye. He fought the urge to run. Valdir said they would be watching Kennard, even over the hill, but Mirella had told him stories about mysterious people and what they did. He put his hand back so his wrist touched the hilt of his short sword.

Slowly, Margali rose, looming over him. He took a small step backward and slipped. He fell against a snow bank.

Margali sat and made a strange noise. At first, he did not know what it was. She let out a wail and he realized she was crying.

"Afraid of me. Why are they always afraid of me, always push me out. I didn't hurt nobody. Not ever. Not nobody."

Kennard rolled over and crawled to her. "I'm sorry. I'm sorry. I didn't mean to."

Head down, she waved at him. "Go away."

He looked up, remembering his mission. "Why don't you come with me? We have some nice sweets in our kitchen."

"No," she sobbed. "They only pretend to be nice. Then they hurt me, or chase me, or make me go away. Have to stay all by myself...only me and my babies."

Kennard remembered what the kitchen folk had said. "We have rags for your babies. A whole pile. My mother keeps a big pile." He held his hand out even with his waist to show the height.

She wiped her nose on her sleeve. "Rags for babies?"

"A whole pile." He raised his hand a little higher.

"Oh." She stood. "All right. Some thread, too?"

"A whole lot. My mother has lots to spare."

She nodded. Holding her doll close, she followed Kennard up the hill. He took Margali's free hand and held it firmly in his, afraid she would run when they got to the top of the hill and she saw the horses.

But no one was there. Kennard dropped her hand in astonishment. Margali took a step forward and turned. "This not the right way?"

He looked up, down, side to side, and swung around to scan the woods behind him. "I...I don't know."

"Margali," said a voice from below. Kennard turned and saw a woman he did not recognize, kneeling, holding out her arms. "Chiyu. I'm sorry for what I did. I was wrong to turn you away. I love you, Margali. Please come back with me. I'll show you how to sew again, just like we used to."

"Mother. Mother, you come back, I knew you'd come for me. I knew it." She ran into the woman's arms.

Puzzled, Kennard walked down the hill toward them. As he came closer to the road, he saw Valdir and Damon and the guardsmen emerge from the trees. And on his right was his Aunt Ellemir, holding Margali in her arms.

"Yes, you're home, Margali. I'll be your mother now. I'll be there whenever you need me."

The next time Kennard saw Margali was in the Great Hall of Armida. Her hair had been washed and brushed and gathered in the back. Her clothes were clean. But she was not an old woman, as he had thought all along, but a girl not more than a few years older than Lewis. She sat on a large chair, legs tucked under her, sewing her doll. Ellemir sat next to her with her arm around the girl. Valdir read a book nearby.

Ellemir smiled at Kennard as he walked in. The older woman turned to Margali and stroked the girl's arm. "Being important is not being the first-born, or having lots of playmates, or even of having laran. It is to love and to be loved."

"Come and play, Ken," called Dorilys from the hallway. She stood next to Lewis, bouncing a ball.

Kennard found that he would much rather watch Margali work on her stitching.

Valdir looked from Kennard to Dorilys. "He'll join you later, Dorilys."

Lewis and Dorilys shrugged and ran off.

Valdir held out an arm. "There's always room for you here, son. I'll read you and Margali and Ellemir a story. There's one here of a boy who won fame and honor because of his brave deeds."

Kennard climbed up on the chair and looked at the pages over his father's arm as the story unfolded.

Safe Passage

Orain wiped his mouth with his hand. Yes, that was blood on his lip. Touching his forehead gingerly, he felt an egg-shaped bruise beginning to grow. Bending stiffly, he scooped up a handful of snow and held it to his head. He staggered to a tree and sat between two large roots, resting his back against the trunk.

Mhari, his chervine, nosed out grass from underneath the snow nearby. One look at her told him that the bandits had indeed taken everything—his pots, his food, his bedroll, his extra clothes, and, most important of all, the money he had accumulated all summer walking from one village in the Hundred Kingdoms to another. For many years, he had made an adequate living selling wares to farmers, hunters, and craftspeople in the summer, and returning to his home town of Neversin in the winter when the roads became impassable. He loved the wandering life and made many friends on his travels. But through luck or chance, never before had he met bandits that had stripped him of everything. Maybe he was getting too old for traveling, he thought as he touched the bump on his head. Maybe he should have gone off the road when he had heard others approaching, as he had done for safety many times before. But the sun had been shining, his spirits had been high, and he had thought that surely nothing bad could happen on such a fine day.

Now clouds covered the sun. Snowflakes began to flutter down. Painfully, Orain got to his feet. He walked over to Mhari and took her halter, the only thing that the bandits had left. He stepped back on the road.

Which way to go? This was an unfamiliar road, recommended to him by friendly villagers in the last place he had sold his wares because of rumors of fighting—an old blood feud—on his familiar path home. To his left was the way back to the village, more than a day's walk. The other way was completely unknown, except that he had been assured it would eventually meet up with the main north-south road to Neversin. He knew there was no shelter for a long way on the stretch of road he had just traveled, so he gambled on finding shelter soon and took the unknown path.

Fortunately, the bandits had not taken anything from the pockets inside his coat. He switched the halter from one hand to the other as he put on his mittens, and then again as he put on his hat. The snow became thicker and the wind struck his cheeks. He pulled the scarf around his neck to its full width to cover his nose and mouth, but the cold still clawed at his eyes. He bent his head and pressed on, hearing Mhari's breath huffing and puffing behind him.

The wind became more bitter as he walked. Tears from his eyes froze on his lower lids, frost formed on his lashes. More than once he stopped and took off his mittens for a moment to pry his lids open. His teeth chattered and his body shivered. Not even force of will could bring it under control.

At last, the track turned. Mhari stumbled down the steep incline after him. He saw the dark wall in front of him only an instant before he collided with it. Stunned, he rested his face against the wooden boards. When he had recovered a little, he moved around until he found a door. The latch was merely a leather loop around a wooden peg; he fumbled with the thong until it came loose, pushed the door with his shoulder, and stepped inside, pulling Mhari in with him.

He stood shivering as his eyes got used to the dimness. Eventually, he saw some light coming through cracks in the walls and ceiling. He was in a barn. A great mound of hay was stacked to one side. On the other were a number of wooden stalls. Orain could hear the scuffling noises of the animals moving within. He smelled the horses as well as hay and manure.

He led Mhari to the nearest stall, which was empty, and tied her to a post there. He used hay to brush her coat, then put a stack of hay near her to feed on. He walked to the door to push it shut again, and burrowed into the nearest mound of hay. Soon, his shivering stopped. He slept.

He woke to the sound of footsteps sliding on the wooden floor. A slurred male voice said, "Say, where'd you come from? Ooh, look at the horns. You got horns, there, horsie?"

Orain parted the hay around him in time to see a young man in disheveled clothes walk up to Mhari. The chervine, used to strangers touching her, continued dipping her head in the water trough as the man awkwardly stroked her head. The man flinched with every twitch of Mhari's head, as the horns wavered near his face.

Cautiously, Orain crept from the haystack. Every crackle of the straw sounded like an explosion to him, but the man did not turn as Orain tiptoed across the wooden floor. Orain grabbed the man from behind, pressing his thick arm against the man's neck until he fainted from lack of air. Slowly, he lowered the victim to the ground. Spotting leather thongs hanging from a ring, he bound the man's hands and feet, and took a kerchief from his pocket, and tied it over the man's mouth. Stepping back to see the man's face, he recognized one of the bandits who had robbed him.

Orain stepped to the door. The new snow shimmered brilliantly in the light of the early morning sun. He shaded his eyes and squinted to see where the man might have come from. Some distance away was a decaying stone house—not a villager's shack or a great mansion, but a house that a minor lord might have built for himself, to house his family and a small staff of servants. But nothing was moving in the snow-covered yard, or behind the panes of the windows that he could see.

Orain turned back to Mhari. He could take her now and proceed up the road, hoping to find a friendly village where he could work for enough food and supplies to get him to Neversin, but if no such village was nearby, he would freeze or starve before finding one. No, he needed at least a hunting knife and a bedroll if he was to make any progress toward his destination. Crouching low, he scurried across the yard and ducked under a window. Cautiously raising his head, he cupped his hands around his face and peered inside. The room was empty. Head down, he padded to the doorway. The door was cracked open; he pushed it gently and it swung inward, hinges creaking softly.

His heart raced as he stepped inside. Cocking his head to catch any sounds, he heard no voices, but he did hear the snoring and moaning of people in sleep. Treading the wooden floor carefully, he went to the room to his left. Peering inside, he saw several men sprawled on the floor. The odor of sweat and stale liquor reached his nose, as well as the pungent smell of vomit. A man groaned and stirred in sleep. Orain flattened himself against the hallway until the sound died away.

Peeking in again, he saw that his bedroll and pack, and even some of his unsold pots and pans had been stacked in a far corner. In order to get there, he would have to tiptoe past the sleepers. An extra blanket had slipped off of one of the men near the entryway; Orain reached in and wrapped himself up in it, covering his head with a corner. He stayed close to the wall as he made his way across the room. If a sleeper opened an eye and saw him, he might think Orain was merely a companion who had gotten up to find a place to relieve himself.

Hours seemed to have passed before Orain reached the other end of the room; his way had been hampered by sticky wine on the floor, and by sleepers flinging arms and legs in his path as they stretched in their dreams. But at last he was bent over the stack of booty. Orain wrapped one pot in the bedroll—he wished he could take more, but more than one would have clanged against the others—took his pack with his hunting knife, and stuffed his moneybag into his coat pocket. All else of his he sadly left behind.

He shed the blanket at the room's entrance and ran across the yard to the barn. His arms laden, he pushed the door open with his foot, stepped across the threshold....

...and promptly tripped over the man he had tied up. The man had worked his gag loose and was struggling to free himself. Sprawled on the floor, Orain picked up his one pot and swung it over, hitting the man in the head. The blow only stunned him, but that gave Orain enough time to gather his possessions and move out of the man's reach. Scrambling to his feet, Orain went over to Mhari. He pulled down more leather thongs from the hook. After bundling his pack and bedroll and pan, he tied them all onto Mhari's back.

Meanwhile, the man, hands and feet still bound, called out to Orain. "Please! Take me with you! I'm not one of them! I came here to get a horse and escape!"

Orain paused in his task to take a long, good look at the man. "Seems to me that you were one of those who robbed me."

"Because they made me! If I hadn't they would have killed me! Please! I'm Jarrel, son of Lord Valdrin! He'll reward you handsomely if you bring me back to him!"

Orain turned back to Mhari. "I thought that Lord Gareth ruled here."

"No! No! The river takes a turn and so we're still in Lord Valdrin's realm!"

Orain turned a skeptical eye toward Jarrel. "In all my years of traveling, I've met smooth liars before, son, and you're not even close to their level."

"No! Please!"

Orain untied Mhari from the post and took her reins. "Please, as in 'please untie me so I can beat you and rob you again'? Sorry, no."

"I swear! By all the Gods, I swear!"

Turning to the young man, Orain tried to appraise his expression. Then he shook his head. "If you really came out here to escape, and not just to water the horses..."

Jarrel's expression changed momentarily; Orain knew he was on the right track. He continued, "...then you will free yourself from your bonds eventually. The bandits inside the house are drunk and asleep. You'll have plenty of time, if you don't cry out."

With the light bundle on Mhari's back, Orain knew that the chervine could carry him easily. He swung up and pressed his knees to her sides.

"I'm your only chance to get away!" Jarrel pleaded. "The others have a sorcerer with them! They'll find you! They'll hunt you! I have a starstone in my pocket! I can help us hide from them!"

"I'll take my chances." Orain guided Mhari to the door carefully; the chervine obediently stepped over Jarrel. The young man screamed after him, confirming Orain's suspicions. He heard other voices answering Jarrel's as Mhari trotted out of the yard.

At first, Orain guided Mhari on the road northeast. Orain reckoned that even roused by Jarrel, the hungover bandits would take some time to come to their senses sufficiently to saddle horses and organize a search party. Still, once he was well out of sight of the homestead, Orain guided Mhari eastward off the road. The chervine could easily pick a path over woodlands that horses would find difficult, and if Orain kept generally to the east and north, he would inevitably reach the main road to Neversin.

He urged Mhari to keep a steady pace until noon, when he stopped to rest and eat. As he was cleaning up, he heard Jarrel's voice shouting, "Hey, pot-man! No escape this time! This time you're dead!"

Orain scrambled onto Mhari's back. To the west, he saw a knot of horsemen through the trees. He knew that any tracker could trace him easily through the new snow, but for horses to follow him through his rugged terrain was nothing less than... magical. He gritted his teeth and urged Mhari forward. He knew little of sorcery, of the laran arts, of the starstone, but he did know that he would not surrender to them again. Maybe they would catch him again, beat him again, rob him again, perhaps kill him. But he was not going to make it easy.

If this had been familiar territory, he could have guided Mhari to a ravine or steep gravelly hill that a chervine could surely cross and a horse surely could not. All he could do now was dig his heels into Mhari's sides, urging her to a gallop, letting her pick her own path. Straight ahead was a thicket. Mhari's antlers barely cleared the lowest branches of the overhanging trees; Orain ducked to keep the leaves from slapping his face. They pushed through the bushes and weeds; suddenly everything went dark. Orain clung to Mhari's neck as she plunged down... what? He could not guess.

They were not falling. Mhari's pace slowed. Orain could feel her picking her way down an incline he could not see. He rubbed his eyes, alarmed by his sudden blindness. Had Jarrel used sorcery against him?

Then Orain saw a thin shaft of light. Looking up, he could see fissures in a stone roof. Slowly the darkness became dimness and he could see the cave around him. Mhari continued to descend along a narrow path. A rock wall loomed up to their left; a deep ravine yawned to their right. Mhari's hoofbeats echoed in the chamber.

Hearing distant voices, Orain turned to the cave entrance.

"You can't get away from us by hiding in bushes, pot-man," called Jarrel. "We...."

Horses and men screamed. Orain heard the thud of solid hitting solid, the scrape of sliding rocks and gravel and the desperate clawing of humans and animals trying to gain a hold on an unforgiving cliff face. The cacophony of sound echoed off the cave walls, then diminished as gravity took hold and dragged the pursuers into the depths.

When it was again quiet, Orain took stock of his surroundings. The path Mhari found was too narrow for them to turn; there was no room even for Orain to step off the chervine and walk alongside her.

"Help," Jarrel wailed.

Orain turned and saw a shadow against the rock face. "I'm sorry," he called softly. "I can only move forward myself."

"Please," begged the young man.

"If you truly have command of sorcery, now is the time to use it," suggested Orain.

"I made that up to get you to untie me."

Orain nodded to himself. "I thought you might have. And told me a tale about being Lord Valdrin's son."

"A lie. Please," he urged. "I can't hold on much longer."

"I couldn't reach you even if I tied all the thongs I have together and threw a line to you. All I can do is go forward and see if I can find a spot wide enough to turn around."

"Hurry."

Orain urged Mhari forward at her own pace. He half-hoped not to find a wide spot, because the bandit would certainly rob him again once free from the fear of death. Then again, Orain needed to find his own way out.

At last, Mhari stepped on a ledge. Orain turned and heard other voices at the cave entrance. He froze. If these were more bandits....

A sorcerous blue light illuminated the cave. Five men stood just at the edge of the abyss. One knelt and held a hand down to Jarrel.

"No tricks when you get on your feet, bandit," said the rescuer. "There are twenty more of Lord Gareth's men just outside."

Jarrel scrambled to solid footing and pointed at Orain.

"Him, too! He's one of us! He forced me to steal! Kidnapped me from my home."

Orain remained still. Sorcery or not, he did not think they could reach him if he stayed where he was.

The rescuer snorted at Jarrel. "You must be the one who claims to be Lord Valdrin's son. Too bad you got greedy and strayed from your own land. Your companions would still be alive if you had known of these caves, and we would not have caught you if you had not left such a wide track through the snow." The speaker pushed Jarrel out of the cave. Then he turned to Orain.

"Come out, traveler. You're safe now."

The man with the stone in his hand that radiated the blue light turned to his companion. "Rhodri, I recognize this pot-seller. He came to my village once a year when I was a youth."

With more light to see by, Mhari reached the cave entrance quickly. Lord Gareth's men followed him outside.

Rhodri looked up at Orain and patted Mhari's side. "You have a good companion here. And here, too," he added, pointing to his head. "Not many escaped both the strength and the wiles of these bandits. If a beating does not work, all they have to do is mention sorcery and their victims do as they wish, not knowing that sometimes even sorcery may be outwitted. I have followed a trail of victims from here to the river."

Orain nodded. "Aye, and I know it."

Rhodri reached for the reins of a nearby horse. "We can take you as far of the borders of Lord Gareth's land. Then you'll be on the main road, and I strongly recommend you keep to that from now on."

Orain smiled. "I will, and you can believe my oath on it," he said, following the party out of the forest.

www.ingramcontent.com/pod-product-compliance
Lightning Source LLC
Chambersburg PA
CBHW071409170626
46811CB00003B/1318